SHROUD OF CLEOPATRA

BOOK TWO OF THE RED JAVELIN CHRONICLES

ROSS HARRINGWAY

Omega Press
El Paso, TX

Editor's note: The events in this book occur simultaneously with the events chronicled in the novel Red Javelin

SHROUD OF CLEOPATRA

OMEGA PRESS

An imprint of Omega Communications Group, Inc.

For information contact:

Omega Press
5823 N. Mesa, #839
El Paso, Texas 79912

FIRST EDITION

Printed in the United States of America

OTHER BOOKS BY ROSS HARRINGWAY

FROM OMEGA PRESS

The Clovis Legacy Series

The Forbidden Region
Reign of Death
Shadows in the Dark
Weakness is Provocative
Illusion of Freedom
Burdened with Morality

The Red Javelin Chronicles

Red Javelin

CHAPTER ONE

"I saw death!"

Drew Harrison struggled to restrain the man that was about a foot shorter than he was and easily over one hundred pounds lighter. Harrison tried without success to avoid smelling the foul body odor of the crazed man. He was wriggling, trying to break free of Harrison's grip, foaming from his mouth. His blue eyes were bloodshot. Harrison could feel the irregular heartbeat of the man as he wrapped his arms around him and held him in a tight bear hug. The man kept kicking and moving his head back and forth, screaming the same words over and over again.

"I saw death!"

Harrison pinned the man to the broken paved ground that was covered with thousands of large, uncut diamonds and closed his eyes instinctively when he heard another explosion to his left. The sound of automatic laser rifle fire and the explosions of shoulder propelled R-5 rocket launchers filled the surrounding area. Harrison pulled out some twist ties and secured the crazed man by his wrists and ankles. The man continued his screaming while the carnage of war ringed around their area.

Harrison had observed the man darting out from behind one of the hundreds of half demolished skyscrapers. He acted without regard to his own safety and dashed out from his sniper position and attempted to tackle the man to get him to safety. But Harrison had not anticipated that the citizen was in the middle of a drug binge that robbed him of any rationality.

Harrison heard the words of First Lieutenant James Shigeta in his left ear, "Get back to your position, Lieutenant!"

The members of the Military Intelligence Branch of the Space Command each had microchip receivers surgically implanted in their left inner ears so that they could easily communicate with one another in time of warfare. They had an additional microchip that was surgically implanted into their left wrist as a means of speaking to their team mates. The two implants were much more practical than the civilian holo-coms or the hand held computers. With the microchip in the wrist, Harrison was able to speak to his unit members without fumbling around with any devices, keeping both of his hands free for weapons or hand to hand combat.

"I saw death!"

"Ah, please shut up!" Harrison yelled at the drugged up prisoner.

"Are you speaking to me, Lieutenant?" Shigeta demanded.

Harrison swallowed, "No, sir. This man won't be quiet. Bringing him in!"

A rocket exploded about fifty yards to Harrison's left. He dived on top of the restrained man to cover him from any shrapnel, diamonds or flying concrete. Harrison felt pieces of concrete and synthetic materials fall on his back like hail in a storm. The pieces of rubble that pelted his one piece black uniform were hot from the explosives and Harrison grinded his teeth together in an effort to ward off the momentary pain. He lifted the man up in his left arm and flung him over his right shoulder. Harrison began running toward the several temporary metallic sniper bunkers that were about a hundred yards away. He ran as fast as he could as laser bursts hit the torn ground around his feet. The enemy had spotted him and were firing in his direction.

Harrison ran faster as more laser fire bounced near his feet. He leaned forward, fearing that he would lose his head at any moment. He ran past a twelve foot high pile of uncut diamonds that took up about thirty square feet on the ground. Each of the jewels in the pile was no less than twenty carat weight and some were over eighty carats. Harrison made it to the nearest black sniper bunker which was seven feet high and twelve feet wide. He slid on the left side of the bunker and was safe from the laser fire from his rear. His legs and feet kicked aside dozens of large diamonds that were all over the ground. He looked into the bloodshot eyes of the man that he had saved from certain death.

"You're safe!"

"None of us are safe! Death is here! I saw death!"

More explosions erupted in the distance and Harrison dragged the man by his right arm to the rear of the bunker to avoid the hail of diamonds that were thrown into the air by the detonations. He quickly secured the man to one of the rails on the bunker with another twist tie. As he did so, Harrison noticed out of the corner of his eye that Marine Corps Lieutenant Jake Brown was looking at him from the front of the bunker.

"Drew, are you nuts?" Brown more demanded than asked. "You could have been blown to bits!"

"But I wasn't," Harrison responded and leaped into

the bunker. The front of the bunker had several one inch wide by three inch length holes so that they could fire their sniper rifles at the enemy. Several of the Raumschiffs that had transported the ground crew dropped the sniper bunkers onto the ground so that the MI and the Marines could utilize them as cover from the enemy. Harrison observed Brown and a non-commissioned officer named Kay Light firing sniper rifles in the direction of the eighteen buildings in the distance, approximately two thousand yards away, dropping the rioting civilians one at a time. Harrison located an extra sniper rifle and aimed the barrel out one of the firing holes, took aim and fired at a man charging at their position, splitting the man in half. His upper torso hit the ground and flipped over and over. His legs kept running several steps, as if they believed they were still alive.

Several of Harrison's closest friends were in some of the other bunkers, firing at the rioting civilians in the distance. He and his fellow service men and women had been dispatched by Colonel Jamal Lincoln to put down a rebellion on planet New South Africa. They had been transported to the location of the insurgency by dozens of Raumschiff space craft from the Battle Cruiser *Cortez* and established a perimeter for the ground forces while the smaller Allen Type one man fighter ships streaked the thirty mile radius of the rebellion on the island of Niles. The civilians were moved to storm the government offices on the island and quickly killed all of the loyalists to the Royal Family that they had found in their path. They were able to seize weapons and fought the few planetary soldiers that had the stomach for engaging them. Their numbers grew rapidly and they were able to take the entire island.

Concerned that the small rebellion would spread to the main continents of planet New South Africa, the Glorious Leader ordered that the *Cortez* move in and crush the traitors. Colonel Lincoln dispatched four fighter squadrons under the command of Lieutenants Devin Millard, Paula Vela, Jason Allen and David French to give cover to the ground forces. The larger Raumschiffs were to drop off the sniper bunkers and begin firing R-5 rockets into buildings that were suspected to be housing members of the rebel groups. The pilots had performed their part of the mission with precision and lightning fast strikes. The majority of the buildings that housed the traitors were levelled in the first few moments of the attack.

Harrison and the others on the ground were in the midst of a major laser battle when he saw the drugged civilian running out into the middle of the battle. Now that he was back in the safety of the bunker, Harrison realized that he could have been killed a dozen times over if the rebels had any experienced snipers. Clearly, the insurrection lacked shooters with any talent.

"Drew, are you crazy?" Lieutenant Yuri Gorski asked from the safety of his bunker.

Harrison squeezed off three shots, hitting two rebels in the chest, "I'm fine, Yuri!"

"That was a crazy stunt you pulled," MI Corporal LaShondra Lewis chimed in. She was in the same bunker as Gorski and had wanted to follow Harrison out into the middle of the laser fire. Gorski had stopped her. Lewis and Harrison had been lovers ever since they met on planet New Edinburgh and had been keeping their sexual relationship secret for fear of reprisals. It was against the Code of Military Justice for an officer to sleep with an enlisted soldier. Although officers and enlisted members were sexually active with one another on a regular basis, Harrison and Lewis did not want to be the two that were caught in the act.

"Yes it was, Corporal," Harrison affirmed. "I won't do it again. I promise."

There were five view screens to the left, right and

above Harrison inside the bunker. They each showed a three dimensional angle of different parts of the battle. The views were made possible by hundreds of golf ball sized scanners that had been released by the Raumschiffs. The scanners filmed the events and digitally uploaded the live images to the Battle Cruiser and the ground forces. Harrison noticed that the forty-two Allen Type fighter ships under the command of Millard were firing rockets on a ninety-one floor building in the east of the city. The building took a few dozen hits before it began to collapse on itself. Harrison grimaced when he saw several of the rebels jumping from the burning building to their deaths on the ground below. The sound of the building crashing to the ground was deafening and the debris, dust and materials that were filling the sky reduced visibility for the ground forces. Harrison silently questioned whether or not they were fighting for the right side.

Then came the announcement they had all been waiting for from Lieutenant Shigeta: "All right people, look alive! We got the order to move into the main business district. Captain Ng and Captain Freis will be moving their companies on the left flank. Captain Chevalier's company will move on the middle section. We have orders to secure the right flank of the main city! The Royal Family wants survivors to be made an example out of, so place all of your laser pistols on stun. Move it!"

"This is it!" Brown pulled the strap of his sniper rifle over his camouflage uniform. "Sergeant Major Light! Get the troops ready!"

Harrison addressed his platoon of forty-two MI enlisted soldiers, "You heard the Captain! Meet me at the right flank! Move out!"

Harrison leaped out from the rear of the bunker and onto the rubble filled pavement. He could hear Brown, Gorski and Dominic Andolini barking out similar orders to their platoons. Dominic had been placed up on the rooftop of one of the tallest buildings located on the southernmost point of the island. From that vantage point, Dominic was able to use his skills as a sniper and target rebels that attempted to reinforce the main clusters of people in the business sector.

Harrison found that the dust and debris limited his visibility to about twenty feet in all directions. He could still hear the sounds of laser bursts and explosions all around him. He found his platoon and noted that his platoon sergeant was not present.

"Where is Sergeant Han?" Harrison demanded of one of his squad leaders.

"She was killed sir," Corporal Offut reported, pointing back over her shoulder at the location where their Raumschiff had dropped them off. "It happened just seconds after we landed." Her black one piece uniform was torn over her left shoulder, revealing a cut that seemed to be a near miss from a laser weapon.

Harrison clenched his laser rifle tighter upon hearing the news. He had relied heavily on Han due to her vast combat experience. Harrison nodded, "Set your laser pistols on stun and follow me to the building located at one o'clock. We are going in and take it floor by floor."

Each of his platoon nodded that they understood just before Harrison yelled at them to charge in. Gorski and Brown gave similar orders to their respective platoons and were running across the rubble and mounds of diamonds toward the few strongholds of rebels that remained.

Gorski fired his automatic laser rifle as he ran. He had selected the Breckenridge Corporation laser rifle due to the rapid fire mechanism and for the triple barrel. Each time he pulled the trigger, several bolts of deadly energy shot out from the three barrels in the direction of the enemy. Gorski could not keep count of how many fell before him, their bodies cut into pieces from his accurate shooting. Several explosions erupted nearby as the rebels tried to fight off the advancing soldiers in vain. Gorski cried out as he felt himself lifted off of the ground when an explosive device detonated about five feet from him. Shrapnel and diamond chunks ripped into Gorski's right side, causing searing pain. He flew in the air and miraculously held onto his laser rifle as he impacted the ground and rolled over twice. Fortunately, his thin body armor that was underneath his black uniform absorbed most of the blast. His ears were ringing as he tried to stand but his right leg gave out on him. Gorski fell flat onto the ground, laser fire flying over his head.

Lewis slid down next to Gorski, firing her automatic laser rifle in the direction of the enemy. She quickly looked over Gorski as she sat up on one knee, firing her weapon. She noticed that Gorski's right leg was torn open just above the knee.

"How do I look?" Gorski grimaced.

"I am calling in for a medic!" Lewis yelled over the sounds of the battle.

Gorski smiled at her and noticed that her left shoulder was bleeding. "You're hit."

"It's just a scratch!" Lewis yelled as she kept firing at members of the doomed rebellion in the distance.

Harrison and Brown led their units into the thick of

battle. Each of their platoons killed hundreds of the armed civilians and stunned triple that amount to give the Glorious Leader the prisoners that he had desired.

"It almost isn't fair!" Brown remarked as he shot three men and seven women in the chest with his automatic laser rifle. "They have weapons but don't have any knowledge of tactics!"

"Tell that to Sergeant Han!" Harrison responded.

The two men heard over their ear piece that Captain Freis had been killed by an explosive device on their left flank. Freis had been a well-liked officer. With the report of her death, any pity toward the civilian rebels ended. Brown and Harrison encouraged their units to continue advancing.

At some point, Gorski succumbed to the pain and slipped into unconsciousness. He did not witness how Lewis and Dominic protected him from the constant waved of advancing and retreating civilians. Dominic spent half an hour, knelt down next to Gorski, firing two laser pistols with an accuracy that was unrivaled. Lewis kept applying pressure to Gorski's leg wound with one hand while she fired at the hoard with her laser pistol using the other. The two killed dozens and wounded twice as many than that.

They held their ground until Lieutenant Sheila Lorbek arrived with her platoon and circled the three, firing wildly at the enemy. Lorbek was three quarters human and a quarter Akarzdamedian. She inherited some of the traits of the Akarzdamedians in that she was seven feet tall, stronger than ten men and could run as fast as a jaguar. Her face was more human than the typical Anubis look of the aliens, but her body was lean and muscular. During the battle, Lorbek proved to be a fierce warrior. As the soldiers protected Gorski, the medical team was able to retrieve him from the battle field and get him to safety.

Gorski woke up in a medical bed that was inside of a Super Raumschiff. He could tell by the movement that the space craft was in flight and fighting to break free of the gravitational pull of the planet. He looked around him and saw several other injured MI soldiers and Marines in the other beds. Some were in worse shape than Gorski. A doctor approached him and smiled.

"You were lucky, Lieutenant." Doctor Macinlock told him. "Corporal Lewis and Lieutenant Andolini got you back to us before you lost too much blood. I was able to repair the severed arteries and patch up your leg. You will be fit for duty in about a day."

Gorski sat up and noticed that a few of the female nurses and doctors were looking him over. He attracted a lot of attention due to his part on the Blood Moon. He smiled back at them and then looked back toward Macinlock. "Dominic and LaShondra? Are they okay?"

Macinlock nodded, "Lewis was hit in the shoulder, but it was just a minor nick. Dominic is still down on the planet surface assisting with the roundup of the criminals. Lewis said to give you a message when you woke up."

"Which was?"

Macinlock shrugged, "She said for you to meet her at Take Ten when you got back to the Cortez. Glad you survived, Lieutenant."

"Thanks, doc. I wish I could return the favor to you."

Macinlock smiled, "Well now that you mention it. My daughters are all back on Sikorsky's Planet. Three of them are in their late teens and the rest are in their twenties. They would love it if I could send them a signed holo-pic of you. They were all quite smitten by you and your team on the Blood Moon."

Gorski nodded, "I would be happy to do that for you, doc."

"I appreciate that," Macinlock told him.

CHAPTER TWO

The murders of the Royal Family members on the Island of Niles were a matter that Anastasia Sikorsky took personally. She was a sixth generation descendant of Vladimir Sikorsky and due to her bloodline; she had been raised to lead. Her position on the *Cortez* was the commanding officer of the weapons supplies. But on this day, she had been ordered to command a team of elite Military Intelligence soldiers to investigate a very troubling question. The New South African Planetary Defense forces should have retaliated against the rebellion on Niles. For some unknown reason, the commanding officers of the defense and the civilian Secretary General did not act. Anastasia Sikorsky was ordered to find out why.

Admiral Weems gave her a four level Super Raumschiff with two pilots and twelve soldiers to assist her in the investigation. But Anastasia intended to do more than just investigate. She wanted revenge on the leaders of the planet for failing to lend aid to her relatives. She requested that one of her cousins, MI First Lieutenant Laura Murdock, accompany her on the mission. Murdock was like minded in her anger that the powers that be omitted to act in defense of the Royals on that island.

Anastasia was dressed in a one piece light purple, long sleeved uniform with dark knee high boots and a dark utility belt that held a holster for her laser pistol and a sheath for a twelve inch blade knife. The shoulders had the triangle shaped gold insignia of the Cortez while the collars held her gold rank insignia. Her long hair was rolled up underneath her purple cap.

Murdock was dressed in a similar fashion with the exception of the color of her uniform. Since Murdock was an officer in the MI, she wore a solid black uniform. Her long blonde hair was pulled into a pony tail as she did not like wearing the military issued hat. Murdock was a descendant of the legendary Five Star General Rock Murdock which gave her plenty of attention since Rock Murdock had died three times and returned to life after each death.

The pilots on the mission were Lieutenant Hans Streicher and Lieutenant Junior Grade LeJuana Bolanos. The two were in the traditional astronaut corps one piece dark blue uniforms. Streicher and Bolanos were flying the craft from the upper level pilot section while Anastasia, Murdock and the eleven MI soldiers were in the lower three levels.

Admiral Weems had already contacted New South African United Nations Secretary General Cherri Ul-Radhsuvian to expect the space craft. Weems gave a stern warning to the Secretary General that the ship had best land safely and the crew treated with dignity and respect. Weems was assured that there would be no problems and that the crew would be received peacefully.

Bolanos marveled at the surface of the planet as she monitored the dozen three dimensional tactical displays to her left side. Each of the ten feet tall and two feet wide screens chronicled the live action on the island of Niles as the marines and MI soldiers attempted to crush the rebel forces on the ground. Bolanos whistled as she saw the sparkling surface below. "Is all of that down below really uncut diamonds?"

Streicher nodded, "Yes they are. There's billions of them. No, trillions. When we conquered this planet the entire economic system concerning the diamond trade was changed forever. There are so many diamonds on New South Africa that most women now do not care for them any longer."

"What do you mean by that?"

He smiled, "A few hundred years ago, women had a strong desire to receive diamond rings or other jewelry made out of diamonds. Due to that demand, the price for diamonds was quite high. Then this new planet was invaded by humanity and when we saw that diamonds were more plentiful in the universe than air, the value of diamonds plummeted. It was simple economics of supply and demand. The supply of diamonds increased to such a high level that the prices hit rock bottom. Now stones like jade or sapphire are more valuable."

"I never cared about diamonds," she told him.

"That's because you were not around several hundred years ago. If you had been, you would have wanted one. Okay, heads up. I see the capital building in the distance. You see it?"

Bolanos nodded as she saw the two hundred floor building that towered over all of the other hundreds of buildings in the distance. The tallest building was purple and pink with some one-way glass windows in a pattern that made no discernable pattern. "That is the tallest building I have ever seen."

Streicher laughed, "You don't get out much, do

you?"

"I was pretty sheltered as a child."

Streicher looked her over and paused for a few seconds as he considered his words carefully. "Well then, you might want to stay on board when we land."

"Why?"

"Because what is about to happen will not be pretty."

The two pilots remained silent as they landed the space craft on the rooftop of the purple and pink skyscraper. Before the ship touched the roof, Murdock and Sikorsky had already lowered the rear loading ramp. It clanged on the metal roof as the craft rested in place. Murdock bellowed at the eleven MI soldiers to move out. They ran double time down the ramp, each of them holding laser rifles in their hands, and came to an abrupt stop when they came face to face with several high ranking officers. The eleven soldiers stood at attention and saluted the officers with their right hands and their weapons shouldered on their left shoulders.

Murdock and Sikorsky walked down the black metal ramp looking over the welcoming committee. Standing front and center of the group was New South African United Nations Secretary General Cherri Ul-

Radhsuvian. She was an elderly woman, over one hundred years old, and seemed frail and tired. Standing behind her was the commander of the Planetary Defense, Space Command Admiral Jianna Lin and her executive officer, MI General Aisha Kolver. Lin was human while Kolver was a half human and half leopard hybrid. Kolver's fur was light orange and yellow with black spots about two inches apart all over her body. Her long tail waived freely from the back of her black uniform. Behind Ul-Radhsuvian, Lin and Kolver were a dozen other officers with the ranks of Commander, Colonel and Space Command Captain.

Anastasia hated the human hybrids and had no trust in their commitment to the Royal Family. She drew her laser pistol as she walked toward the assembled officers and aimed at Kolver. Before Kolver could protest or react, Anastasia pulled the trigger, blowing the top of Kolver's head off. Her body spun in a sideways circle before collapsing to the metal roof.

"I hope that got your attention," Anastasia said, almost laughing as she stepped past Kolver's corpse. "I am Anastasia Sikorsky, a proud member of the Royal Family and an officer of the UNSC Cortez. I was sent by my family to determine why your Planetary Defense forces refused to take action against the traitors on the island of

Niles. Anyone care to enlighten me?"

New South African United Nations Secretary General Cherri Ul-Radhsuvian stepped forward to face Anastasia. As an old political veteran, she knew that the Glorious Leader would exact a heavy price from the leadership of the planet. Due to her experience, Ul-Radhsuvian had ordered that some of her officers hide her children and grandchildren from the wrath of the Royals. Understanding she was about to die, she addressed Anastasia with respect, keeping true to her years of diplomatic training.

"Welcome to New South Africa. We are humbled and elated by your arrival."

"Sure you are," Anastasia snorted as she aimed her pistol at Ul-Radhsuvian.

The other officers began to move to surround her but stopped in their tracks when Murdock snapped her fingers and the eleven MI soldiers with her aimed their laser rifles in their direction. "I suggest that each of you officers stand down while we investigate the criminal violations of treason that have been committed on this planet."

Admiral Lin refused to cooperate with Murdock's demands. She growled and leaped in the direction of

Murdock. Stepping to her left, Murdock delivered a right hook into Lin's jaw, sending the Admiral sprawling to the metal rooftop. Murdock began kicking Lin in her mid-section and ribs, her metal tipped black boots ruptured Lin's spleen and cracked several of her ribs. Lin cried out in agony with each impact as Murdock showed no signs of letting up on the onslaught. The other officers were frozen in fear, unwilling to act to assist the Admiral. Lin was spitting up blood as she tried to get to her hands and knees. Murdock delivered a kick to Lin's face, breaking a few teeth and sending the Admiral flailing back to the metal roof.

Lin stopped moving, lying in a pool of her blood as she whimpered in pain. Like the Secretary General, Lin had sent her children into hiding to avoid the inevitable death that awaited them all. Her last thought was her hope that her children had been able to make it to a safe refuge. She made no sound as Murdock shot her in the back of the head with her laser rifle. Lin's head was obliterated and the others stared at her headless body with dread in their eyes.

"Now, will there be any other idiot heroes here?" Anastasia asked the others. "Let me size up where we are. Traitors rebelled on Niles, killed members of the Royal Family and then declared their independence from the

Glorious Leader. The Planetary Defense is mandated to crush such rebellions. Admiral Lin did not act as she was required under the Code of Military Justice. Why?"

A Space Command Commander raised her hand and waited until Anastasia pointed to her. "Admiral Lin ordered us to stand down. We wanted to attack, but Lin told us that a heavy handed invasion of Niles would be counter-productive."

Anastasia nodded as she listened to the officer in dark blue. She smiled and faced her, "What is your name?"

"Commander Trizhia Cort."

Anastasia motioned with her laser pistol, "Commander Cort, please come over here and stand by my side."

Cort dutifully walked over next to Anastasia and stood in silence, her head down as she could not look her fellow officers in the eyes.

Anastasia pointed at the secretary general and the other officers as she spoke to the eleven MI soldiers next to Murdock. "Kill them all, except for Commander Cort."

"What? But it was Lin that made the decision to stand down! We are all innocent!" Ul-Radhsuvian raised her voice as she protested the order.

Anastasia shrugged as the eleven MI soldiers aimed

their laser rifles at the officers, "That's what they all say. Lin violated the Code of Justice and ignored her obligations. Each of you could have arrested Lin and relieved her of her duty. But, you did not and you sealed your fate by your omissions to act. Fire at will."

The MI soldiers began firing. The officers tried to run, but were each cut down by the rain of laser fire sent in their direction. Anastasia and Murdock waited patiently as the officers fell, one by one. Ul-Radhsuvian died when a laser burst ripped through her chest. She crumpled to her knees and fell face first onto the rooftop.

When it was over, Anastasia faced Cort. "Looks like you are now in temporary command of the Planetary Defense of New South Africa. We will be leaving these eleven MI soldiers with you and a few well trained officers to back your play. Unlike Lin, they understand their sworn duties under regulation. I assume there are children of these dead officers?

Cort nodded.

"Good. Your first duty as CPD is to track down the offspring of these traitors and eliminate them all. Do it publicly, crucify a few dozen children, burn a few to death, maybe have some of them raped. Have news crew present when you kill them so that all of the citizens on the rest of the planet can witness the fate of any that dare question the Glorious Leader. Also, make sure you take a few heads and post them over the doorways of some of the main governmental buildings. It will act as a deterrence to anyone that might be considering rebellion. You see, it is easy to gamble with your own life. But when you gamble with the lives of your offspring, well, that is a different analysis entirely." Anastasia motioned for the eleven soldiers to accompany Cort. "My commanding Admiral will be sending in a few officers to assist you in bringing order back to this planet. All hail the Glorious Leader."

CHAPTER THREE

Several days after the mission to planet New South Africa had been completed, Marine Corps Colonel Jamal Lincoln took time to enjoy his day off from duty. Commander Cort had graciously given Lincoln several platoons of soldiers from her forces to replace the ones that had died on the island of Niles. In return, Lincoln sent Captains Chevalier and Ng to assist Cort as the new command staff for the New Planetary Defense. He also sent a Super Raumschiff filled with prisoners from the rebellion to stand trial on Sikorsky's Planet.

Lincoln had gone to the gymnasium and completed a two hour work out then ate a good meal at the officer's cafeteria and then settled in at his quarters to relax for the evening. He had picked out two old movies to watch from the computer archives. Exercise and movies were the way Lincoln had found were the best for him to relieve the stress of his command.

Lincoln was the commander of the United Nations Space Command Battle Cruiser *Cortez*. His crew of about one thousand five hundred men and women had been depleted due to the mission to the island of Niles. Lincoln had put off the unenviable duty of dictating holographic messages to the families of the crew members that had died in the line of duty. He calculated that he had lost two hundred eighty-three crew members, including Captain Freis and six junior officers.

The adults on the vessel were either military service or in the civil service as civilians. The spouses that were on board were also required to work. No free rides were permitted by the United Nations Code of Military Justice. Some of the families had children on board that were required to be indoctrinated by the teachers in the day care facility. Lincoln had been given the command of the *Cortez* three years ago. It was a rare thing for a Marine to be given the command of a space craft as those positions were generally reserved for Space Command astronauts. But Lincoln had distinguished himself in battle and he had taken many computerized classes to learn all he could of space warfare. His research papers on military tactics had padded his resume and brought his name to the attention of the ranking officers from the Security Council. Admiral of the Fleet William Sikorsky had personally promoted Jamal Lincoln to Colonel and assigned him to act as Captain of the massive war ship.

Lincoln's Captains quarters was decorated with Medals and written letters praising him for past acts of heroism. He had pictures of his children on the walls as well. There were pictures that had Lincoln with his deceased wife hanging next to those of his children. She had died many years ago and Lincoln had never remarried. Being a single father and a commander of a Battle Cruiser was enough work to occupy a full day. Accordingly, he had little time to meet and romance a new lady. His oldest child, Mary Johnson Lincoln, had recently graduated from Clovis Academy and volunteered to serve on a mission in the farthest reaches of space. She had always been daring in that manner. His other children were in Universities around the universe. Each had chosen their own path to follow in life, which was exactly how Lincoln and his dearly departed wives had taught them.

Lincoln poured himself a whiskey and water and then sat down on his bed. He ordered his computer to begin showing the original version of "The Manchurian Candidate" on his big three dimensional screen. The movie began and Lincoln relaxed, taking a drink and forgetting his daily troubles.

After about fifteen minutes the computer alerted Lincoln that he had an incoming communication from the Space Command. It was Admiral of the Fleet Sikorsky. Lincoln hid is drink behind a desk and asked his computer to pause the movie. Lincoln sat up and faced the camera on the wall which would send his image to the person he would be conversing with. If the Admiral of the Fleet was contacting him directly, there must be a serious mission about to be assigned to the *Cortez*.

"Display three dimensional broadcast," Lincoln instructed the computer. He watched a life size image of the ranking officer for the Space Command materialize before him. He loved the advanced technology that his ship had recently been given. The communications were now so clear that it was as if the person he was speaking with from the distance of dozens of Astronomical Units away was standing before him. Lincoln felt as if he could touch the image before him and it would be a real person as opposed to a holographic image.

"Colonel Lincoln," Admiral Sikorsky greeted him.

"Admiral," Lincoln saluted him. "How can I serve the Space Command this morning?"

"Colonel, we know you are in route for planet

Cootron to pick up supplies and then back to Mars rendezvous with the rest of your fleet," Sikorsky began. "First of all, I wanted to let you know that the Glorious Leader is grateful for how you handled the rebellion on the island of Niles. Unfortunately, we need to call upon you and your crew once more. We need you to divert your flight and investigate something for us. Your Battle Cruiser is the closest war ship to the last location of the Eighth Fleet. I have distressing news that had to be given to you and you alone. I trust no one else is in your quarters?"

"We are alone, Admiral." Lincoln confirmed.

"Good. This is top secret information. We have lost contact with all five of the Eighth Fleets' Battle Cruisers."

"That is Rear Admiral Cardenas' Fleet?" Lincoln asked.

"Yes. Cardenas and his Fleet were escorting several dozen large transport ships full of civilians that were enroute to settle on several planets and moons we had successfully Terra-formed. Their last stop was to be on planet Cootron. About thirty days ago, we lost all contact with the entire Fleet." Sikorsky told him.

Lincoln paced in thought, "All five ships? What about their coded transmission beacons? Did those cease to work as well?"

"All five and yes their beacons stopped transmitting about the same time we last heard from them. That means that the ships were all destroyed or someone knew how to bypass the beacon security systems and disable them. Either way, it is not a set of facts that we need to be admitting to. Civilians want to feel safe and knowing that five Battle Cruisers are gone without explanation could cause a stir with the people. Especially since we are having so many pocket rebellions breaking out. Jamal, these ships were traveling together on the same mission," Sikorsky affirmed.   "Are there any intelligence reports from the area of space that they were passing through?"

"None."

"No clues as to whether or not the Fleet was attacked?"

"We have no information whatsoever. I could spend the next few hours speculating as to what might have happened. The truth is we are sending your ship in with hopes that you can report the answers to all of your questions back to us."

"Understood, Admiral."

"Jamal, we cannot allow this information to leak out to the public. The Sixth and Seventh Fleets disappeared many years ago. That has harmed the public perception with regard to our ability to defend our planetary holdings. Losing the Bismark was also a public relations snafu. The public trust in the military is at an all-time low. Only bring in your most trusted crew as to this secret."

"You can count on me, sir," Lincoln assured the Admiral.

"I know I can, which is why this assignment had to go to you. Your ship is one of the finest in the Space Command. Find the Fleet and Cardenas. Report to me directly. We need to know exactly what happened and why they cannot respond to us. I fear the worst."

"We will make haste to their last known position. I will only bring in my top officers and Admiral Weems."

"Good. Thank you for your service, Jamal. Admiral Sikorsky, signing off."

Lincoln sat in silence for a few seconds. He recovered his drink and finished it in one gulp. He reflected a moment on the words of the Admiral. The level of discontent among the civilian population seemed to be rising ever since the Blood Moon Incident. Lincoln had heard reports of unrest in certain areas. Planet New Berlin had reported numerous riots in the streets against the Glorious Leader and his family. There were intelligence broadcasts indicating that the moon named Chronos was in danger of seceding. He walked to his closet and asked the computer to open the door to reveal his many military uniforms. He had several Class A dress uniforms for ceremonies and greeting dignitaries and higher ranking officers, his Class B standard outfit for everyday use on board the Battle Cruise and the Class C uniform which was generally used for combat. Lincoln began changing into one of his camouflaged Class C uniforms.

"Computer," Lincoln said as he found his black boots and began pulling them on over his feet and over his ankles. "Notify Admiral Weems to meet me in the Executive Conference Room on Deck Five, say in thirty minutes. Also inform Captain Sowa, Lieutenant Commander Marywood, Lieutenant Commander Tony Allen, Lieutenant Shigeta, Lieutenant Laura Murdock, Doctor Taejo Jin-Woo, Professor Simon Brennan, Doctor Henri Malvaeux and Doctor Erik Macinlock that their presence is requested."

"Notifications have been sent," the computerized voice answered.

"Thank you." Lincoln felt odd thanking his computer. But he did so out of courtesy and habit. He brushed his teeth and rinsed his mouth out with breath freshener. He then walked to one of his several desk drawers and opened it. Inside were numerous weapons of differing sizes and make. Lincoln lifted up a web belt and strapped it over his shoulders and waist. He began affixing hand lasers and stun darts to the belt. He took out two knives and attached them as well. His greatest fear was of the unknown. If another alien race had ambushed the missing Fleet then they could be lying in wait for the rescue mission. Lincoln wanted to dress with as many weapons on him as possible so that his top ranking crew members would understand their new mission was not a drill.

It was the real thing.

He had known Admiral Cardenas for years. If something had happened to Cardenas and his fleet, then everyone venturing into that sector of space had best be prepared for anything. Lincoln was not going to take any chances with his ship or his crew. He decided that they would fly at best speed to investigate what had caused Cardenas' Fleet to cease contact with the rest of the Space Command. The secondary part of the mission, Lincoln felt, was to avoid the same fate for his own ship and crew.

Take Ten was one of the many restaurant/bars on board the Battle Cruiser *Cortez*. Take Ten was the most popular among the single and available members of the *Cortez* crew. It was a well-known location to meet others for romance and or sexual escapades. The Bar was run by several human bartenders and many more robot servers. The robots were all eight feet tall, silver in color, with eight arms and four legs each. They were able to carry multiple trays of food and drink and service many tables at the same time.

The crowd at Take Ten was bustling, many service members and civil service crew were there, eating and drinking. There were only a few open tables.

Drew Harrison was a newly commissioned Second Lieutenant in the MI Branch and had just survived his first action on the island of Niles. He was enjoying his day off from duty, sitting at a round metal table eating a sixteen ounce rib eye steak with sautéed mushrooms, a baked potato, steamed broccoli covered with melted cheese and an ice cold pint of beer. Harrison was wearing his standard issue solid black Class C fatigues. He was one of the tallest men in Take Ten. His bulging muscles were hardly concealed by his uniform.

Sitting next to Harrison was Corporal LaShondra Lewis, his secret girlfriend. Although the UN Space Command publicly frowned upon officers fraternizing with enlisted personnel, in reality it was allowed. Lewis had met Harrison when she was working as a body guard for one of

Harrison's female friends at the Clovis Academy. They became lovers soon after meeting one another. When Harrison joined the crew of the *Cortez* as his first assignment, Lewis requested and received a transfer to join him. Lewis was also eating a steak, although much smaller than the one that Harrison was enjoying. On the table top was a small pile of uncut diamonds that Lewis had brought back with her as souvenirs of their time on New South Africa. Lewis was not the only crew member that had helped themselves to some of the diamonds on the planet surface. Each of the survivors of the ground invasion had stuffed a few of the lovely jewels in their pockets or web belt packets so that they could send them off to some loved ones on other worlds.

Also at the table were MI First Lieutenant Laura Murdock, Marine Recon Lieutenant Jake Brown and Space Command Pilot, Lieutenant Paula Vela.

Murdock was about five feet seven inches tall with blonde hair, blue eyes and slender body. She was considered by many to be one of the most attractive women on the Ship. Murdock was wearing the same solid black uniform style as Harrison and Lewis to signify that she was in MI. Murdock had been in the military service for five years and was third in command of Military Intelligence on board the *Cortez*. Murdock had achieved her education at the Academy on Sikorsky's Planet, earning her doctorate in Criminal Investigations. Murdock was also a seventh generation descendant of the Glorious Leader, Vladimir Sikorsky, but she kept that fact to herself. She wanted to be accepted by her crew mates for her abilities, not because she was a member of the Royal Family.

Paula Vela was about five feet two inches tall, with dark hair and olive colored skin. Her eyes were light brown. Her uniform was a dark blue signifying that she was in the pilot corps. Her long sleeves had a red stripe circling her wrist cuffs which signified she was also a search and rescue expert. Vela had attended the Academy in Santiago, Chile, graduating with Honors. Vela had been in the service of the Space Command for seven years and hoped to one day soon be promoted to Chief Pilot on a Battle Cruiser. She had been submitting her requests to be considered for promotion for the past year whenever an opening would be advertised. She had received several rejection letters. Each correspondence only motivated Vela to apply more often.

Brown had a shaved head as was the norm for the men and women that were members of the Recon elite. He had brown eyes, stood about six feet tall, muscular and had a chiseled jaw. He had been a member of the *Cortez* crew for two years and commanded a platoon of Marine Corps soldiers. He also worked on security for the ship. He was married before joining the service but his wife had never joined him. She had recently informed him through an attorney that she was seeking a divorce. Brown was generally quiet, especially while eating. There was a sixteen ounce T-bone steak and baked beans on a large platter before him.

Both Murdock and Vela were enjoying bowls of Tortilla Soup and drinking ice water. Although the two women were not on duty, they were on "Skeleton Crew" duty, which meant that if someone scheduled for duty did not report, they could be called to fill the shift.

Murdock had become acquainted with Harrison and the new officers in the Military Intelligence section of the Battle Cruiser *Cortez*. Murdock had already probed Harrison regarding the famous battle at the Moon orbiting planet Semiramis. Vela had not had that opportunity.

"So, Lieutenant Harrison," Vela said loudly over the low roar of many other tables of conversations occurring at Take Ten, "Everyone on the ship is talking about you and Gorski. What you two did on the Blood Moon has grown into the stuff of legend. What is it like to be a famous person? I mean you are a celebrity."

Harrison had gotten several similar questions since the incident on the Blood Moon. He was not even certain how he felt about what had happened. "Please, call me Drew. What is it like to be famous? I am not sure." He paused to drink a sip of beer. "I can tell you this, I am just happy to be alive. We all could have died out there. We were alone, outnumbered, out-gunned and we survived only because we fought for it. We out worked the assassins. We prepared for them while they rested. How does it feel?" Harrison shook his head. "I miss Porfirio and Pierre. I will always feel sad that they died on that moon and left behind children. I guess I just don't really like to think about it."

Vela nodded. She knew Harrison was referring to cadets Pierre Zerbe and Porfirio Cardenas. Both of them had died in the attacks. Vela felt awkward for having brought up the subject. She took a spoon full of her soup in her mouth and swallowed. She decided to change the subject.

"So what was the deciding factor for you to apply for MI?" Vela wanted to know.

Harrison shrugged, "My best friend, Yuri, was the one that thought it would be the best course for us. I just took his advice. Speaking of Yuri, where is he?"

"Late as always," Lewis observed. Yuri Gorski

always seemed to be ten minutes behind, no matter what the occasion. But it was never due to Gorski procrastinating. He was one of those men that kept his calendar full.

"But Gorski was also a good pilot," Vela observed. "By joining MI he won't be able to pilot any ships."

"Gorski was one of the best pilots from his graduating class," Murdock added.

"But his father is a Marine," Harrison pointed out. "Both his parents were and they were Spetsnaz graduates. Yuri was one of two graduates from Clovis Academy to attend the Spetsnaz training. So, Yuri wanted to put that expertise to its' best use and join MI."

"There they are!" Lewis said with a tint of excitement in her voice.

Across the room, near the entrance of Take Ten, stood Yuri Gorski and Dominic Andolini. Both men were wearing their Class C solid black MI uniforms. They were looking around for Harrison and the others. Gorski was a muscular man, handsome with grey eyes. Gorski had been one of the heroes of the Blood Moon incident. He had taken over leadership of the Clovis Academy team when the selected commander was seriously wounded by a Saharakaree. Through Gorski's leadership, eight cadets stood up to incredible odds and won the fight. Gorski had been single for the last few months as his last love interest, Jen Staszko, had decided to call off their relationship after he had graduated from the Academy. Gorski was one of the playboy single officers on the *Cortez*. He had been dating a nurse, a computer technician and an enlisted Marine. Gorski had been instructed by Jen Staszko to live his life. He had not hesitated to take her advice, sleeping with several women on the ship. His most recent conquest was a nurse that had assisted in treating his injured leg. After they had made love, the nurse left his room quickly as if she were embarrassed by the fact that she gave her body to him so easily. Gorski wished that the woman had stayed and spent some more time with him as he had found her to be quite pleasing in the bedroom. He had memorized her name and promised himself that if time permitted, he would seek her out for another session of raw passion.

Dominic was from a very large Italian family. He had many siblings as his parents believed in creating many offspring. Dominic had an identical twin brother, Marco, who had been assigned to serve as a pilot on a different Battle Cruiser. Dominic was slender, most likely due to all of the running he did from his years of playing intramural and professional futbol, also known as soccer. He had been a star on the Clovis City soccer team and led his team in scoring. He had dark hair, brown eyes and a brilliant smile. He was also a deadly marksman. He had spent years honing his skills with hand lasers, laser rifles, knives, cross bows, bows, spears, rifles, pistols and various other weapons. After settling in on his first assignment as an MI officer on the *Cortez*, Dominic began studying for a law degree using computer lectures and materials. His gold wedding ring was on his left ring finger. Before leaving the Academy on Clovis City, Dominic married the love of his life, Cadet Harumi Shigeta. His spouse was still attending the Academy and finishing her education. Fortunately, their separation would only be for a year. Once Harumi graduated she would be able to join him at whatever post he was serving at that time. Many of the female crew members had made passes at the young officer only to be turned down. He would show them his wedding ring and tell them that although he was flattered by the attention, he had to decline due to the love he felt for his wife. Loyalty to his friends, family and his wife was perhaps his best character trait. Dominic also was a person that had a zest for life and he took a keen interest in befriending others. He would always greet people with a sincere embrace.

And today was no different. Dominic was hugging

many people in the crowd at Take Ten, knowing all of their names. He would introduce Gorski to other crew members; most of them were individuals Gorski had never seen on the Battle Cruiser *Cortez*. Gorski was always amazed how Dominic could meet so many people and remember their names, their spouses and children's names.

To the right of the entrance to Take Ten, there was a large party of about thirty officers, all wearing dark blue to signify the Space Command Branch, toasting one of the group.

"That's the going away party for Lieutenant Jason Allen," Dominic observed as he and Gorski walked through the crowd to get to the table where Harrison, Lewis, Murdock and Vela waited. "He just finished his six year obligation to the Space Command."

"Allen?" Gorski looked over to the group of pilots. "Is he from the Allen family?"

"Yes," Dominic pointed in the direction of Allen. "Next to Jason is his older brother, Lieutenant Commander Anthony Allen. He is second in command of the Pilot Corps on the Cortez. Remember we met him when we came on board the Cortez? Marco mentioned that he had met him after you were all rescued on the Blood Moon."

"That's right, I remember him." Gorski recalled

meeting Allen when they were preparing to send the body of Zerbe to the surface of the gas giant Osiris.

Gorski noted that the two Allen men were tall, slender, and handsome and seemed to be popular with their peers. Gorski saw Lieutenant Junior Grade Frank Glenn celebrating with the Allen brothers. Glenn had attended Clovis Academy with Gorski, Dominic and Harrison. Glenn had graduated a year before they had and was assigned to the *Cortez*. Gorski had always been on good terms with Glenn as they had been fairly close friends for the three years they were cadets together. Glenn had already been given the opportunity to serve on the Command Station of the ship as pilot and in the Astral Navigation position. Gorski had always respected Glenn and was happy to see that his career was advancing so well. Glenn had recently become a father for the second time. His wife, Orallia Li, had given birth to a boy to go along with their twin girls from a year ago. Glenn made eye contact with Gorski and waived at him. Gorski smiled and nodded in his direction to indicate that he saw him. With Glenn and Li on board with Gorski, Harrison and Dominic, that totaled five Clovis Academy graduates on the ship.

Dominic made it to the table of Harrison and the others first. He began giving his customary greetings, in the form of strong hugs, to Brown, Murdock, Vela, Lewis and Harrison. Gorski shook their hands.

The two men sat down with the group.

"I probably should go and say my good byes to Jason Allen," Vela observed. "When we make it to the next Space Station he will be leaving the service and going home."

"And he really is a member of the famous Allen family?" Brown said for conversations sake. "The Allen Corporation family?"

Murdock nodded, "Yes he is. Most of the Allen family go to a military academy, serve six years, and then go home to help the Corporation design and build ships, weapons and work on medical advancements."

"If I had their money I doubt I would want to start off my service as a front line junior military officer." Harrison commented.

Gorski recalled the small fighter ships that stock all of the Battle Cruisers and Academies as being produced by the Allen Corporation. And then there was the metallic arm that Elektra Papanikolaou had been given after she lost her limb in the fight against the Ragnarsson assassins. The mechanical arm, which looked like her real arm, had been created and designed by the Allen's.

"I don't know about that, Drew." Gorski said thoughtfully. "Traveling around the solar systems might be the best way for an up and coming corporate captain of industry to learn things. Think about it. They will know other cultures, other worlds and meet people from other socio-economic backgrounds to broaden their view of the universe. They might be in a better position to relate to others by serving in the military before they embark on managing a multi trillion dollar a year company."

"We have a friend back at the Academy that hated the Allen's," Harrison recalled. "Remember, guys? Dirk hated them."

Dominic chuckled at that as he waved for one of the robot waiters. "That was because Dirk's family and the Allen's were in competition with each other."

"What family was your friend Dirk from?" Vela was curious.

"He is from the Fenster family," Gorski said and then ordered a pitcher of beer for the table from the robot waiter. "He said that there was bad blood between the two families."

"I say," Murdock pushed her empty soup bowl aside. "After the murder that was never solved. I bet the Allen and Fenster families would kill each other if they were ever alone together in a room."

"What murder?" Lewis raised her eye brows at that. She was always wanting to keep up on the news. The fact that there was a murder mentioned that she had never heard about was enough to pique her interest.

Murdock looked at the others, surprised they had never heard the story. "About twenty years ago, the oldest Allen arranged for his grandson to marry a Fenster girl. It was like a Royal Wedding. Two of the wealthiest families on all of the settled solar systems of Earth were going to be joined together by marriage. The news media, paparazzi, commentators, members of the Royal Family, elected leaders from the UN and nosey spectators were all over the wedding location in upper New York. The Glorious Leader sent several of his wives and children to attend the event. All of the Fenster and Allen family were in attendance. But just before the ceremony was to begin, the bride to be, Iridia Fenster, was found hacked to death at the church. She was in her wedding dress, covered in her own blood. The Fenster's blamed the Allen's for the murder based on their belief that the Allen member did not want to marry her. The police investigation cleared the Allen's of any wrong doing, but that did not dissuade the accusations from the Fenster's. The police spent tireless hours looking into every possible lead, but her killer was never found. The rift between the two families created by the accusations and the murder has grown over time. The Allen family and Fenster family will never collaborate or cooperate again. The whole thing was just very, very sad."

"What happened to the groom to be?" Vela prompted.

"He is a Captain of a Battle Cruiser somewhere." Murdock frowned, trying to remember where he had ended up. "He wanted nothing to do with his family business after he lost Iridia. I think that he really loved her."

"So for him it was not just an arranged marriage," Harrison concluded. "That explains quite a bit regarding Dirk's hatred for the Allen's. I guess Iridia would have been Dirk's aunt."

"And the murderer was never found?" Gorski shook his head. He was taken aback that he had never heard the story from Dirk. Normally, he was an open book with all of his friends. He rarely hid things from them. Gorski wondered why Dirk never opened up to him about his family background more. The two men certainly shared many drinks together over the two years they knew each other. "With the money those two families have, they couldn't hire the best investigators and solve the crime?"

"They tried to solve the crime," Murdock told them. "But there were no clues left behind at the scene. No DNA evidence was found at the crime scene. No fingerprints. No eyewitness accounts of any unknown persons sneaking into Iridia's waiting chamber at the church. No security cams to catch anyone going in or out of the bride's chambers. Nothing. The perpetrator may still be out there somewhere."

Murdock intentionally held back the rest of what she knew. As a member of the Royal Family, Murdock had been made privy to the behind the scenes truth regarding the murder of Iridia. The Glorious Leader did not want the two powerful families united. To avoid the union of the two groups, Sikorsky had sent in assassin Dell Ragnarsson to kill Iridia. Sikorsky was cognizant that her murder would have the potential to cause the two families to hate one another. Murdock dared not share that fact with anyone, especially the three men that knew one of the Fenster family members.

Gorski leaned forward, looking into Murdock's eyes, with a smile on his face. "The only crime here is that we have not slept together yet."

Murdock smiled back at him. Gorski had been trying to bed her for the last few weeks and she had been playing with him, never agreeing but flirting back to give him that glimmer of hope that it might happen. "I out rank you, Mister. I have already told you that I don't rob the cradle."

"There is only a few years difference between us." Gorski was still smiling at her. He was very attracted to Murdock. Since his longtime girlfriend, Jen Staszko, had ended their relationship, Gorski had been looking for a new woman to spend time with. There were plenty to choose from on the Battle Cruiser *Cortez* and Gorski had taken a few women to his bed. But he was drawn to Murdock as she was one of the more attractive single ladies of the crew.

Murdock had decided she would eventually give in to Gorski's advances, but she wanted him to suffer. She wanted him to grovel to get her into his bed. Murdock found that because of her looks, her body and her sex appeal that she could easily break men. She received a sadistic pleasure in doing so. As part of her efforts to lure men, Murdock intentionally had her MI uniforms altered to fit her tighter in the chest and leave little to the imagination. She would often times put on her class C uniform without wearing a bra so that when she was in some of the colder areas of the ship, her nipples would harden and attract attention. She was resolute in her decision that Gorski would be her next victim.

Vela stood up as she was uncomfortable with the sexual tension between Gorski and Murdock. Based on past history, Vela knew that Murdock was toying with Gorski. Vela and Murdock had served together on the Cortez for the last five years and she had learned from past history the manner Murdock used men. Vela had become friends with Murdock, probably best friends, and each woman confided in the other over the years. Murdock generally used men and would toss them out of her life like yesterday's garbage when she was done with them. When Vela first met Gorski, she would attempt to get his attention as a possible romantic partner. Unfortunately for Vela, Gorski had his sights set on Murdock from day one. Vela confessed to Murdock her attraction to Gorski and urged Murdock to make certain Gorski understood he had no chance with her. Murdock refused Vela's request as she found pleasure in stringing him along. "I, um, I am going to say farewell to Jason. I will see you all next time."

Vela left the table and joined her fellow pilots across the room. She hugged Jason Allen and told him she wished him the very best in the future. The younger Allen graciously thanked her. As Vela walked to the exit of Take Ten, she reflected back to the time she first joined the crew of the Cortez. She and Jason had been young graduates when assigned to be pilots on the large Battle Cruiser. Vela had developed a crush on Allen at first. But Murdock got Allen's attention first and started sleeping with him. In a few months' time, Murdock ended her involvement with Allen to pursue another crew member. He had been devastated by the break up and became fairly reclusive. Vela wondered if Jason was leaving the *Cortez* because Murdock had used him like she had done to other men. Now Murdock had her designs on Gorski and Vela wanted to warn him, but she concluded he was a grown man and he had to make his own decisions.

Lewis, who was a computer broadcast news addict, had her hand held computer device on the table. The others were talking about the convictions on Clovis City against the Blood Moon conspirators. She had heard the same conversation from Harrison and Gorski in the past and had tuned them out as she read the current events on the twelve inch wide and eight inch high holographic screen before her. Her eyes went wide when she saw the headlines of the dead Chronosians. "By the Stars!"

"What's wrong, honey?" Harrison saw that Lewis was clearly disturbed.

"The moon, Chronos, one of the ones orbiting

Osiris?" Lewis looked up from her small computer, her eyes wide with disbelief. "Some weapon hit the moon. The news reports all eight hundred thousand colonists were killed. There were no survivors."

"My God," Dominic said under his breath. Osiris was the largest planet in the solar system where planet New Edinburgh was located. He imagined that his friends at the Academy, his wife, siblings and parents were able to see the blast from their home telescopes. "Was there any clue as to the cause?"

Lewis shook her head from side to side, "None that had been reported. But wait! It seems the Glorious Leader took full responsibility, he referred to all of the citizens as traitors."

"So he wiped out almost a million people?" Harrison blurted out without thinking. He quickly remembered that he was in Take Ten, a public gathering place and that he should mind his words carefully.

Before any further comments could be made by the group, the ship computer began making an announcement. "The following personnel and officers are to report immediately to the Executive Conference Room: Captain Sowa, Lieutenant Commander Marywood..." The list of names continued.

When Murdock heard her name announced, she stood up and smiled at the others at her table. "Duty calls. I bet this has to do with the Chronos explosion. Until next time?"

Gorski watched as the desirable Murdock left the table. Gorki was admiring the rear view of her as she walked away.

Harrison was watching Gorski's eyes. The friendship between the two men was strong enough that Harrison could tell by the look in Gorski's eyes what he was thinking. "Yes, my friend, she is a tasty looking morsel."

Lewis punched Harrison in the chest. There was clear anger in her eyes. She was jealous that her man would complement another woman like that. "And what am I?"

"You are the main course," Harrison responded before he kissed her in an attempt to diffuse her hostility. "You hit hard."

"Keep staring at other women and I will hit harder." Lewis warned him.

Dominic watched as the robotic waiter returned and began pouring beer into individual glasses for the occupants of the table. He felt sick to his stomach. Almost a million lives snuffed out in seconds. He looked at his full glass of beer, trying to make sense out of such a horrible act. He wondered who would create such a weapon of mass destruction and what kind of twisted mind would even contemplate using it. The fact that the two hundred forty-one year old Vladimir Sikorsky took credit for the slaughter was equally disturbing. While he was fighting the rebels on the island of Niles, Dominic had questioned whether or not he had been on the right side of the conflict. Now his crisis of conscience was growing given the slaughter of so many.

"Dominic, hey!" Gorski hit the Italian on his shoulder. "You are staring out into space. Are you okay?"

He nodded, "Yeah, I am fine." He picked up his glass and drank some of his cold beer. He wanted to leave, to go back to his quarters and contact his wife, his parents, his siblings and his twin brother Marco. He had a strong need to hear their voices and tell them how much he missed them. "How's your leg?"

"Good as new. Doc Macinlock fixed me up."

CHAPTER FOUR

Admiral Burton Weems had been in the employ of the United Nations Space Command for many years. At age twenty-two he had graduated from the Academy in Heidelberg, Germany and was commissioned as an Ensign on the historic Battle Cruiser called *Bismark*. As a member of the Flight Corps, now called Pilot Corps, he quickly rose up in rank. Within two years he was promoted to Lieutenant Junior Grade and a year later to Lieutenant. He became one of the more talented flight officers in the service. By his sixth year, he was transferred to the Battle Cruiser *Arizona* as Chief Pilot as a Lieutenant Commander. By his twelfth year in the service he was promoted to Commander and assigned as the Executive Officer of the Battle Cruiser *Waterloo*. In his sixteenth year of service he returned to the *Bismark* as her Captain. He served in that role for ten years before accepting a promotion to Admiral. Now, at age fifty-eight, Weems was the Admiral of the

Fifth Fleet. He was responsible for managing the crews and inventory of five Battle Cruisers. One of the ships in his Fleet was the *Cortez*.

Weems had his offices on board the *Cortez*. Weems had every confidence in her Captain. As a result, Weems rarely took part in the day to day operations or missions of the ship and focused more on screening graduating cadets for possible selection to serve as part of the crew. But on this occasion, Lincoln had requested that Weems join the top officers of the ship to staff a potential mission.

Weems entered the large Executive Conference Room to see that Lincoln was already present. The two men greeted each other with handshakes. The rectangular table, which was capable of seating up to fifty individuals, had two other crew members present. Captain Mara Sowa, chief of the MI branch on board the *Cortez* was seated at the far end. She was wearing her solid black Class C uniform. She smartly stood to attention when the Admiral entered the room. Sowa was an exemplary officer as she never had any disciplinary issues and her section was run well. She was also the chief of the Criminal Investigation Division on the ship. She supervised ten officers and a few dozen enlisted men and women. Sowa was married to Doctor Laurent Sowa, who was the commanding medical officer on the Cortez. They had two young children together that were generally raised by the day care employees on the ship.

Weems motioned for Captain Sowa to sit.

The second crew member that was present was Doctor Taejo Jin-Woo. He was a member of the non-military civil service and the chief Engineer of the *Cortez*. Normally a civilian was not allowed to be in charge of a section aboard a Battle Cruiser, but due to Jin-Woo's knowledge and experience, Colonel Lincoln was able to convince Space Command to make an exception. Jin-Woo looked like an old school heavy metal rock star, with his uncombed long black hair with streaks of grey that fell well below his shoulders. Jin-Woo was not very tall, standing at just a tad over five feet. He was wearing light colored pants and a purple turtle neck sweater. He nodded to the Admiral when he noticed his presence. Jin-Woo had never found time to marry, but had three children, all by different women, scattered around the Eight Solar Systems. Jin-Woo would joke that each time he published a new manual on engineering the proceeds would go to pay his back child support.

Lieutenant Commander Clarissa Marywood, Lieutenant Commander Anthony 'Tony' Allen, Lieutenant

Jim Shigeta, Lieutenant Laura Murdock, Professor Simon Brennan, Doctor Henri Malvaeux and Doctor Erik Macinlock all entered the Conference Room together. They were all early. The motto of the Space Command was that if you were not fifteen minutes early, you were late.

Marywood was the Chief Pilot of the *Cortez*. She had served in that position for a few years now. She had recently been passed over for promotion to the rank of Commander to fill the position of Executive Officer of another Battle Cruiser. It was the first time she had applied for such a position and normally it would take a few more attempts before she was promoted. Admiral Weems had written a letter of recommendation for Marywood as he felt she was prepared to take on a new challenge in her career. Marywood later learned that she was not selected because one of the Sikorsky great grandchildren received the position in her stead. She had always suspected that nepotism was the manner in which promotions were handed out by the Space Command. She was not the first to be overlooked for a position that went to a connected Royal Family member and she was certain she would not be the last.

Anthony Allen, who preferred to go by Tony, was the second in command of the Pilot Corps. He was also the

Commander of the Search and Rescue unit. He had eaten a few breath mints to cover up the alcohol on his breath from the celebration he attended at Take Ten. Allen was from the wealthy and famous family that owned and operated the Allen Corporation. Due to his love of the service, he had shunned the demands of his family to leave the Space Command after his sixth year of mandatory service as an officer. Allen stayed on, finding solace in flying space craft in the eerie silence of space. Participating in corporatism was not a life that he desired. His plans were to stay on the *Cortez* and work to obtaining his own command one day, just as one of his uncles had accomplished. Allen was wealthy due to his shares of stock in his family business. He had over five million Empire Dollars' worth of shares in his portfolio and a tad less than that amount in cash.

Jim Shigeta was the second in command of MI and of CID. He came from a sibling group that was scattered throughout the many settled planets of the Eight Solar Systems. His sister, Harumi, was married to Dominic Andolini. Shigeta had lobbied Weems to select his brother-in-law to serve on the *Cortez*. Weems agreed when he reviewed Dominic's proficiency scores in marksmanship. Shigeta was in top physical condition and one of the best at breaking down a potential suspect in the interview room.

He held a Master's Degree in Criminal Investigations and a Doctorate in Weaponry. He was more than qualified to rise up the ranks in the service. He was also well trained in hand to hand combat as well as several martial arts.

Professor Simon Brennan was a brilliant Astro-Physicist and probably the one person that Lincoln admired most on the ship. Thus, Lincoln sought out Brennan's advice and counsel often. Brennan had wanted to retire for many years, but Lincoln would convince the older man to stay. Brennan was wise, calm and thoughtful. His experience had made him a valuable part of the crew. He had married twice and lost both wives to tragic accidents. He had two children with his first wife that were teachers on planet New Berlin. His second marriage produced a daughter that had attended the famed Sikorsky's Academy and became a pilot. She vanished as a member of one of the lost fleets.

Doctor Henri Malveaux was a brilliant Bio-Chemist that was generally invited to meetings in which theories of phenomena were needed. He was the opposite of Brennan in personality. Malveaux was arrogant, short tempered and combative at times. If he had not been so knowledgeable, someone might have thrown him out of an air lock years ago. Malveaux had several wives and numerous children.

He had also been a lover to Laura Murdock some years back, a fact that Murdock never allowed Malveaux to forget whenever she needed favorable treatment from the science section.

Doctor Erik Macinlock was a medical doctor. He had joined the crew a few years ago and saved Admiral Weems life during open heart surgery. Macinlock was well liked by the crew. He had been one of the men that Laura Murdock seduced and slept with. Murdock would occasionally show up at Macinlock's quarters and sleep with him. Before becoming a medical doctor on board the *Cortez*, he had worked on secret research projects for cloning, limb replacement, DNA splicing, genetic alterations of fetuses, and mind pattern transference. He was a widower; his wife had died ten years ago when she was caught in the crossfire of a laser shoot out on Earth. His children were all living on Sikorsky's Planet, some already in careers and some were attending a university in the highly populated London City.

After the prestigious group had settled into their chairs, Lincoln called upon the ship computer to display in the middle of the rectangular table the pictures of the Battle Cruisers in the Eighth Fleet. Next the three dimensional images of the five ships were pictures of each ships'

Captain.

"This is top secret information. Each of you know from your oaths to the Military Code that sensitive information cannot be discussed to anyone outside of the hull of this space craft." Lincoln began, feeling a bit redundant in repeating standing orders that he was certain that his top staff officers already knew by memory. But the regulations required him to remind the crew members of the law whenever some sensitive intelligence was about to be shared. "I received orders from the Admiral of the Fleet to investigate why the Eighth fleet has lost contact with the Empire. As you see before you, we have five Battle Cruisers, under the command of Admiral Cardenas. His flag ship is the Cleopatra. The other four Battle Cruisers are called the New Hampshire, Stirling Bridge, British Columbia and the Tonkin Gulf. All five ships have ceased transmissions.

"The Eighth Fleet was escorting scores of transport ships to several lunar colonies and then to the ultimate destination, planet Cootron. Those ships carried thousands of citizens that were to occupy a newly constructed city on Cootron. The transports also had enough supplies, livestock and provisions so that the settlers would be well off."

"So what happened to the Fleet?" Captain Sowa cut

in.

"A few days ago, Cardenas and his Captains no longer responded to the daily communications from Space Command, as is required by regulation." Lincoln answered her. "We all know that Cardenas is not a man to ignore regulations. He is a highly decorated officer and has served the Space Command with honor and distinction. His five Captains, Faisal al-Bashir, Natalia Sikorsky, Arvidas Sikorsky, Thomas Tsukifuji and Trini Urbanczyk are also failing to respond to requests from the Space Command. Naturally, the Admirals are greatly concerned about this."

"Especially given the mass murder on the Moon Chronos," Jin-Woo was nodding his unkempt dark hair.

"Yes, that is a fear, that somehow the events are related to something much larger. With New Berlin citizens rioting as we speak and some on old Earth demanding cessation, the Admirals are worried that if this leaks out it will embolden those that are leaning toward insurrection." Lincoln acknowledged to the staff. "Simon, I need you to confer with Dr. Macinlock, Professor Malveaux and Doctor Sowa to prepare all necessary scans to determine if this was an attack. If we find them, I want those five Battle Cruisers checked for radiation, strange life forms, and hull breaches, signs of internal or external attacks, diseases and even food poisoning."

"What are our orders?" Weems asked.

"To immediately search for, locate and intercept the five ships and find out what happened to them and their crews," Lincoln responded. "Tony, I know your little brother Jason was scheduled to depart tomorrow when we were to dock at the next space station. I need you to ask him to stay on for a few weeks more. Once we find out what has transpired we will get him back to Earth."

"Thank you Colonel," Tony Allen said. "I will explain it to him. He is a good team player. He will understand."

"I need all of you to be tight lipped about the mission," Lincoln warned. "If word gets out that this Fleet is missing or damaged, it could harm morale throughout the Eight Solar Systems. The people need to feel as if they are being protected by the greatest military ever. We have already lost the Bismark and two other Fleets over the previous few years. So, secrecy is critical at this point. Tell your sections that we are going on some new training mission."

Brennan cleared his throat, "If we do not give our

first responders complete information, and a potential threat still exists on those vessels, would we not be adding to their potential danger?"

Lincoln sat down next to Brennan. "When we arrive at the location of the ships, that is if we even find them, we will then hand pick the teams that board those ships. And yes, my old friend, we will give those men and women complete disclosure at that time."

"So our orders are to plot an intersect course to the last known location of the Eighth Fleet and make best speed to that location?" Marywood asked.

"Those are your orders," Lincoln answered.

Marywood stood up, "Permission to be excused so that I may take command of the flight controls and plot our interception course."

"Permission granted," Lincoln told her. "This meeting is over for now. I will be meeting with many of you individually to give you separate instructions."

The men and women at the meeting all began to stand up. There was work to be done.

Astronaut Jason Allen took the news that he would have to remain in the service a few weeks longer in stride. He did not let minor setbacks stress him out too much. Plus, he was only leaving the service out of loyalty to his family. His preference would have been to continue as an officer. He enjoyed being a part of the flight squadrons on the *Cortez*. The camaraderie he shared with his fellow pilots was something that he cherished. He especially enjoyed spending time with fellow pilots Vela, Glenn, Aceto and Millard. They were all good pilots and they shared qualities that most pilots had such as the lust for fast speeds, adventure and the adrenaline rush when they had to maneuver between tight spots. But, he was an Allen. He had a duty to the family to return home and learn the corporate business.

Dominic took time to relax in his quarters before watching a three dimensional view of a law professor lecturing on the topic of offer and acceptance in contract law. He heard his buzzer from the entrance go off about twenty minutes into the lecture. Guessing that the person at the door had to be either Harrison or Gorski, he instructed the computer to open the door. He looked over his right shoulder to see the doors at the entrance of his quarters slide open. He watched with confusion as Laura Murdock walked into the foyer. She was dressed in a white half shirt that was tight fitting around her breasts and a pair of pink cotton pants. On her feet were some white slippers. She had a bottle of red wine in her right hand. She walked toward

Dominic as the door slid shut behind her.

"You study way too much," Murdock told him as she approached him. She stood for a moment in silence, observing the image of the law professor in the center of his room, speaking in a monotone voice about the concept of consideration in a contract negotiation. "I brought a bottle of Merlot, imported from Earth. It was quite expensive. I think you will like it."

Dominic stood up and asked the computer to pause the lecture broadcast. He was not sure of what to make of Murdock's sudden appearance at his door. She had normally interacted with him as a superior officer would normally do so with a junior officer. For Dominic, that was fine by him. Although she was a very desirable woman, He had learned as a professional soccer player that woman such as Murdock would come and go. He failed to understand why his friend Gorski was wasting so much time on her when she was clearly a woman that was out for herself and had an agenda behind her every action.

"What can I do for you, Lieutenant?"

Murdock smiled and set the wine bottle on the night stand by Dominic's bed. "I think you should be asking what we could do for each other. Out here in space, people can get lonely. Spending time, enjoying a member of the opposite sex, is a fantastic way to avoid the boredom. Come on Dominic. All you do is study, study, study and then you go to the gym and then to the weapons section for target practice. That isn't entertainment. I can show you a much more thrilling way to pass the time."

Dominic realized Murdock was making a pass at him. He could see that her white half shirt was made from thin material which left little to the imagination.

Seeing his eyes wander to her chest Murdock smiled. "You like my melons?"

"Excuse me?" Dominic was looking at her eyes now.

"My breasts. My tits. I would like to see what it is like to have your hands on them."

"Laura, you know I am a married man," he shook his head 'no.'

Murdock sat down on his bed and stretched out. "And she is how many Astronomical Units away? Come on, Dominic. No one will ever know. Come on. I never had the chance to fuck a true sports star."

"I will know," he said as Murdock pulled off her half shirt, exposing her bare breasts to him.

"How can you say no to a set of tits like mine?" Murdock lay down on her back and smiled at him. "Come on. This is the easiest piece of ass you will ever get. Take me."

Dominic walked over to his door and pointed at it, "I have to ask you to leave. Please."

Murdock sat up, frowning. His reaction was unexpected as she had never been rejected before. "No man tells me no. I promise you will enjoy it."

"Please go," Dominic told her. "My wife may be far away, but I love her. I am sorry to disappoint you, but I will not do this to her or to myself. She means everything to me. Please leave."

Murdock stood up abruptly and pulled her half shirt back on. "You are only tossing me out because your wife is Shigeta's little sister. If you were married to some other girl, you would be fucking me right now. Dominic, you are making a big mistake by throwing me out of your quarters. I have powerful friends and they could help you advance in your career. But if you want things between us to be like this, then so be it."

She glared at him as she stormed out of his room. He noticed she had left the wine bottle behind. He shook his head.

"At least I still have some sex appeal left," Dominic muttered to himself. He returned to his holographic lecture and quickly put Murdock out of his mind.

Murdock was furious. She had never been denied by a man before. She had even succeeded in seducing many married men with little effort. She walked briskly down the hallway of the housing section for officers. She came to the quarters of Gorski. She stopped and stared at his door. Murdock was in need of a man, any man, to make love to her. She knew that Gorski wanted her. Her plan had been to make him wait, to beg for her to become her lover and then enjoy watching his pain after she dumped him.

But Murdock's sex drive took over.

She pressed the button on Gorski's outer door, letting him know that he had a visitor outside. Gorski had just returned to his quarters from a two hour work out at the ship gymnasium with Harrison. Gorski and Harrison had spent almost every other day at the Academy working out together. They had carried over that comradery to their assignment on the Battle Cruiser *Cortez*. The two men challenged each other to push themselves. The time at the gym was always fulfilling for both. After the work out, Gorski had returned to his quarters and showered. He was wearing a pair of cloth shorts and a t-shirt from Clovis Academy. He had just sat down on the floor of his room to clean his weapons when he heard the chime from his door.

He had not been expecting any company. He ordered his room computer to open the door to whoever was outside.

Murdock waited as Gorski's doors slid open. She saw him sitting on his floor, cleaning a laser rifle. Murdock walked in slowly and smiled as Gorski stood to meet her. She rushed into his arms and began kissing him. He responded by kissing her back and running his hands over her body.

Gorski was not certain as to why Murdock had decided to change her mind about becoming involved, but he was elated she had. The two removed one another's clothing quickly. Murdock allowed Gorski to pick her up in his arms and carry her to his bed. As he ran his hands over her naked body and kissed her all over, Gorski realized that Murdock was probably the most physically desirable woman he had ever held in his arms. He determined to make love to her slowly, not rush things. He wanted to savor every second of having her in his bed. They made love and fell asleep in each other's arms.

Gorski had been the first to doze off while Murdock lay still in his arms. Most of her lovers would be so full of lust for her that they would not last long before climaxing. Gorski had been different. He made love to her in a way to ensure it would be pleasurable for her. Murdock rested her head against his muscular chest and closed her eyes. She decided that it might be a good idea to keep him around for longer than she had originally planned.

CHAPTER FIVE

Professor Simon Brennan checked over the stellar cartography pictures in the large observation deck of the Cortez. He had been directing the scientific and technical staff to scan the last known location of the Second Fleet. They had found no clue as to the missing ships. Brennan then instructed the staff to scan the regions around the last reported areas to determine if the fleet had drifted in space.

And they were somewhat successful.

Brennan inspected the photographs that revealed two of the five missing Battle Cruisers and several of the missing civilian transport ships. There was no evidence of floating debris as one would expect from a space craft that had been destroyed. Brennan deduced that meant the other three Battle Cruisers were off in some other location.

Brennan ordered the photography team to continue their work and expand the search outward another ten degrees circumference. He left them to go and report the findings to Lincoln and Weems personally. As Brennan walked out of the stellar charting auditorium, he was suddenly seized by a flash of pain in his left side. He leaned against the wall, holding his stomach with his left hand. The pain subsided after a few seconds. He caught his breath and vowed to go see Doctor Laurent Sowa later to be examined. Brennan had suffered the shooting pain before and had put off seeking treatment.

The Weapons Section of the *Cortez* was vast. It was the size of two football fields and was located on what was termed the Second Level. It was nicknamed the "Peace through superior fire power" room. The Marines and technicians that worked in the Weapons Section were able to fight a battle using the on board laser weapons, armor piercing rockets, pulsar blasts, and long range missiles. Also at their disposal were weapons for defensive use, such as counter-measures which were pieces of scrap metal to throw off metal seeking or heat seeking projectiles. The weapons could be fired from the left and right of the *Cortez* as well as the front and rear.

In a side section of the same Level on the ship was the vast storage room. It had high ceilings and metal floors with racks and racks of armament. The storage area had four offices, some computer terminals and about one hundred square yards of floor space. The quartermaster of the storage area was in control of all of the ship's laser rifles, hand lasers, cross bows, knives, stun darts, flame darts, body armor, helmets, shoulder operated rocket launchers, land mines, explosives and other various items for hand to hand combat. The quartermaster of the *Cortez* was also the second in command of the weapons section. Lieutenant Commander Anastasia Sikorsky had joined the crew of the *Cortez* three years earlier to fill that slot at the bidding of her great great grandfather, the Glorious Leader Vladimir Sikorsky.

Anastasia was in her early forties, but looked like she was twenty. She proudly wore her light purple uniform each morning as she supervised her office. She kept a tight rein on her inventory of ammunition and weaponry, requiring that the men and women under her command to keep strict sign out sheets of any and all personnel that check out items. She would generally work ten hour days, hoping that would demonstrate that she was a dedicated officer to Lincoln and Weems.

She also used her storage area for the weekly meetings of the Royal Family members that were serving on board the *Cortez*. Anastasia sent the two Marines that were assigned to work the morning shift with her to an early lunch. Sitting alone in her weapons storage, Anastasia waited for her family members to arrive to discuss any and all new events affecting the family. The first to walk into the storage area was her uncle, Commander Ervin Urbanczyk, the Weapons Chief of the U.N.S.C. *Cortez*. Urbanczyk was in his eighties, but due to harvested body parts and stolen skin from younger humans, he looked about forty years old. He had metallic bones and younger men's muscles mended into the alloys. His skin was from several young men that were flayed alive so that Urbanczyk could live longer. He nodded to Anastasia and sat down next to her.

The next to join them was Doctor Laurent Sowa, the chief medical doctor on the *Cortez*. He was dark skinned, clean cut, slender and spoke with a deep voice. His features were pleasant and he walked with confidence. He was wearing a medical outfit and had a hand held computer-projector in his left hand. Sowa was the point man for the Royal Family. He was the one that the Glorious Leader and his children would contact with news or orders.

"Good morning," Doctor Sowa greeted his two family members. He looked around the empty chairs and his demeanor changed, he was grinding his teeth. "Where are the others?"

"We are the first two to show up," Anastasia told her two uncles. As she was speaking, Laura Murdock and Lieutenant Jerry Goodman entered the spacious storage room and nodded to the others.

Goodman was an engineer under the command of Doctor Taejo Jin-Woo. He was tall and lanky. He walked with a limp from a leg injury he suffered the previous month. He had not shaved for several days and his hair was greasy due to a lack of showering. He covered his bad body odor with expensive colognes. Urbanczyk glared at Goodman, disapproving of his appearance.

The five sat down in chairs and rolled them into a circle. Doctor Sowa laid his computer projector on the metal floor and instructed it to show the pictures that the Admiral of the Fleet had sent to him in an encrypted message. The other four Royal Family members gasped as they were treated to three dimensional gruesome images of family members' headless bodies.

"Someone is targeting us," Sowa said softly. "We have lost over two hundred family members and the body count is certain to rise. The Glorious Leader thinks it has to be some individuals higher up in rank, an Admiral or General that deduced that we place family members on each ship, planet, moon and space station to maintain control. The perpetrators have killed all of our family representatives on a fleet of science vessels surveying some of the Outer Regions of space."

"What are our instructions?" Urbanczyk wanted to know.

Sowa looked at his fellow Royal Family members. "We are to start taking control of the ship, subtly. Our leaders think that the missing ships from Admiral Cardenas' fleet are connected to these murders. We could have people on our ship that will start targeting each of us to cut off our heads, very soon. So, I can tell you that I have already begun the process of solidifying our power on the Cortez."

"What specifically have you done?" Anastasia asked.

"A few months back I put a brain neutralizer microchip in my lovely wife's brain," Sowa told them. "She is the Security and MI Chief and a confidant of Lincoln and Weems. Once I remote activate the neutralizer in her head, I can control her completely. She will do and say whatever I instruct of her. With her under our thumb, we will have a voice in the inner circle. I have also administered slow poison on the dear Professor Brennan at his last physical. We all know he is the closest advisor to Lincoln. If Brennan is dead or incapacitated, then Lincoln would be forced to seek advice from another source. Perhaps one of us."

"Good thinking," Urbanczyk nodded. "Anastasia and I have the weapons area and storage units secured. If anything happens, we can control all of the offensive weapons on this ship. If we need to, we can blow the whole ship to hell from this location."

"I have slept with several of the officers and have a few tied around my little finger." Murdock smiled. "If need be, I can get a few of them feuding. One or two might be willing to kill one of their romantic rivals for me."

Goodman laughed, "Just give me the word and I will slit Jin-Woo's throat and take over the life supports systems. If we take that section, no one will be able to oppose us."

Sowa nodded, "Anastasia is Lincoln still giving you the eye when you are near him?"

"Yes," Anastasia said slowly, wondering what Sowa had in mind.

"Good, seduce him." Sowa instructed. "Get him to fall in love with you. If Lincoln has you close to him when I finish off Brennan, you could be that close confidant to help us. Are you up to it?"

Anastasia glared at Sowa, "I am a Sikorsky. A little sex for my work and family might be enjoyable. I will make sure that Lincoln will be eating out of my hands."

Sowa turned to Murdock. "So, who do you think you could manipulate into killing for you? I am very interested in that subject."

The Command Station of the *Cortez* was bustling with activity. Lincoln was seated in the Captain's chair. Next to him in the Executive Officer's seat was Admiral Weems. Several feet in front of the two men were the pilot and astral navigation controls. Lieutenant Vela was seated at the Astral Navigation next to the pilot for the shift, Frank Glenn. There were two armed Marines at the elevator lift entrances keeping guard. On the first balcony operating the engineering controls was Lieutenant Danica Garcia and seated next to her was Captain Mary Sowa who was in charge of security. On the second balcony there were three civilian computer technicians and one Marine Corps officer for the weapons controls.

Lincoln and Weems stood expectantly when Brennan entered the Command area.

"Simon? What have you found out?" Lincoln inquired.

Brennan produced the photo imaging print outs to the two men. "We found only two of the five Battle Cruisers. One is listing in space and it seems that it has been damaged. The second is floating aimlessly. There were also several of the civilian Transport vessels in the vicinity."

"Any signs of life forms?" Weems was looking over Lincoln's shoulder at the images.

"None," Brennan told them. "If there are any people on any of those ships, they are dead. We saw no evidence of debris or wreckage. So the other missing ships are still out there, somewhere."

By now, Captain Sowa had descended the metal ladder from her balcony station and was standing next to the three men. "At best speed, how long would it take us to get to their location?"

"Ma'am, I can get us there in a day and a half." Vela spoke up.

Lincoln nodded, "Do it. Direct course."

"Yes sir," Vela smiled at Frank Glenn and whispered to him. "You have to speak up to get noticed, Frank."

"So you have told me," Glenn whispered back to her. The two began programming their interception course and Glenn began to direct the ship with the red glowing holographic half-moon steering column toward the coordinates of the floating ships.

Lincoln sighed, "Simon, let's get the executive team assembled to the meeting room. It is time to organize search and rescue teams to board those two battle cruisers. We will need to brief the teams as to the situation."

"Full disclosure," Brennan smiled.

"Nothing less," Lincoln smiled back at him. He turned and faced the rest of the crew. "Lieutenant Vela. The command officers will be retiring for a confidential meeting. Would you please take command of the Cortez?"

Vela gave Glenn a controlled smile and then stood to attention. "With pleasure, Colonel."

"You are in command," Lincoln told her as he led Sowa, Weems and Brennan toward the elevator lifts. "Have Lieutenant Jason Allen report for duty and take your station at Astral Navigation."

"Yes sir," Vela said as she carefully sat down in the Captain's chair. It had been her lifelong dream to command a ship of her own. She leaned back into the chair and smiled. It felt great to be in the seat.

Clarissa Marywood joined Doctor Taejo Jin-Woo, Captain Mara Sowa, Doctor Laurent Sowa, Commander

Ervin Urbanczyk, Anthony Allen, Brennan, Lincoln and Weems in the Executive Conference Room. They all sat close together at the rectangular table.

"What is going on?" Marywood was not in uniform, wearing a pair of shorts, tennis shoes and a red t-shirt. She had been in the middle of a kick boxing class at the gymnasium.

"We located two of the battle cruisers," Lincoln told her. "I was promised by Lieutenant Vela that we could be at their location in a day and a half. So, I want to have two Super Raumschiffs prepared with a full search and rescue crew on each. Their mission is to board each of the two abandoned battle cruisers. I want everyone to keep in mind that these missions are top secret and each member we select must be trusted. Tony, who are your best search and rescue pilots?"

Allen cleared his throat, "Lieutenants Vela and Streicher, sir."

"Okay," Lincoln nodded. "Inform the two Lieutenants to prepare Super Raumschiff's Cortez 7 and Cortez 14 for first contact with a derelict vessel. Captain Sowa, we will need a platoon of Marines and some military intelligence soldiers to go on each ship."

Sowa tapped her fingers on the table, "I lead one platoon on Cortez 14 with Lieutenant Andolini and Sergeant Major Light. I will have Lieutenant Shigeta lead the team on Cortez 7 with Lieutenant's Gorski and Harrison."

"I will put together a team of four engineers for each ship," Jin-Woo told them. "I will lead one mission and Lieutenant Garcia will lead the second."

"Medical?" Lincoln looked over to Doctor Sowa.

"I will put together a team of nurses and lead one group and have Doctor Macinlock lead the second."

Lincoln looked over the group, "We all know the lesson of the Argonaut from many years ago. We send in robots first to scan for traps, dangerous organisms and life forms. Once the robots clear the lower levels, the engineering teams can commence trying to fix the ships. Simon, I would appreciate it if you would go along with one of the teams and get Professor Malveaux to fly in with the other ship. We don't know what we will be facing over there. Tell the selected teams to be on their guard."

All of the Executive Team had been instructed during their required staffing as to the *Argonaut* tragedy. The Space Command had implemented new protocols that had to be followed strictly to avoid a repeat of that event. Lincoln and Weems made it clear to the entire boarding team that they expected those regulations to be followed.

Drew Harrison had been summoned for duty by Captain Sowa at a highly inconvenient moment. Harrison had been in bed with LaShondra Lewis, enjoying making love to her when the command was broadcast through his private quarters' computer system. Harrison groaned and rolled off of the beautiful woman and made his way to the shower in his bathroom.

"Really?" Lewis demanded angrily. She had also been enjoying their intimate contact and was a bit stunned that Harrison would jump for the shower instead of finishing their passion together. "You are just going to leave me like this?"

"Honey, I am sorry, but Captain Sowa said for me to report ASAP." Harrison told her. He pointed at his bathroom. "You can join me in the shower?"

Lewis sat up in the bed; her angry eyes looked sexy to Harrison. She said nothing, jumped to her feet and met Harrison in the bathroom to finish what they had started. They were kissing as he lifted her in his muscular arms and placed her in his shower. He pushed her up against the black and red tiled wall as the water showered down on them from the sprinklers hidden in the ceiling. He mounted her with a ferocity that led her to cry out his name with each thrust. Her toned legs were wrapped around his back as he anchored her in his muscular arms.

"I love you!" Lewis cried out loud as she had an orgasm and buried her head in his chest.

"I love you, too!" He was able to tell her between his pants of passion.

Dominic found solace at the practice firing range on the Second Level of the ship, nearby the Weapons Section. He had developed a habit of spending each morning at either the gymnasium or the shooting range, alternating the two each morning. Dominic had received a long range triple crossbow from his parents as a graduation gift. He had been practicing with the weapon for several months, mastering it. Due to his steady regimen at the firing range, he was now proficient enough with the crossbow to fire all three quivers at a time, and score hits with all of them. He kept himself busy with athletics, weapons training and law studies so that he could be the best that he could be and due to his loneliness without his wife, Harumi.

This particular morning, Dominic was angry. He had just spent twenty minutes in a person to person satellite conversation with his wife. She had informed him of the death of Lupita Calderon and the apparent kidnaping of Dirk and Therese Fenster. He recalled the Calderon girl as being sweet and kind, although he had never been particularly close to her. That was mostly due to the fact that several of the Calderon brothers had been members of the Bragg Gang and natural rivals to the members of the Gorski Gang. But Dominic had been close to Dirk, good friends in fact. Other than a pissed off Bragg Gang member, Dominic could not think of anyone that would want to kidnap the Fensters.

Anastasia Sikorsky had watched the Italian on several occasions when he would spend an hour or so at the practice range. She had concluded that Dominic was one of the best marksmen she had ever seen. He was nearly perfect with a hand laser. He rarely missed when he would throw knives at the human replica targets. And now he could hit three targets at the same time with his crossbow. Anastasia determined that Dominic was a man that she needed on her side, when the eventual conflict came.

She approached him and introduced herself to the man, "Hi, I'm Ana."

"Yes, ma'am," Dominic stood to attention, seeing her high rank on her shoulder.

"At ease, soldier," she giggled. "No ranks in the

firing range as far as I am concerned. Can you teach me how to fire that, what is it called?"

He handed her his crossbow, "Absolutely I can teach you. That is, if you have the time. I am sure a person in charge of the weapons inventory is very busy."

Anastasia took the weapon out of his hands, "Quit being so formal. Call me Ana." She inspected the crossbow, aiming down range at the colorful bull's eye targets. "Show me how to load it."

Dominic smiled and took the weapon from her and began to lecture the Sikorsky woman on the fine art of safety, loading, aiming and firing a crossbow. For a moment, she was able to divert his internal anger over the taking of the Fenster siblings and the murder of Lupita.

Anastasia handled the crossbow in both of her hands. As he gave her verbal instructions on how to load and fire the weapon, she placed a small brown piece of magnetic tape on the right side of the crossbow. The tape had a computer micro-chip inside, smaller that a grain of sand, which acted as a homing beacon. She smiled pleasantly at Dominic as he showed no signs that he had detected her duplicity. As long as the microchip was attached to the crossbow, Anastasia would be able to track it for a ten mile radius.

She paused when she heard Captain Sowa's voice come over the ships' broadcast system. She specifically requested that Andolini and others report to the Docking Bay within the hour.

"Duty calls," Dominic told her. "Would you like to borrow it and practice?"

"No," she smiled, handing him back his crossbow. "I am clumsy and lose things. Next time you come to practice, come by and get me at my office and I will learn more about how to use it then. Good luck at the Docking Bay meeting."

"Thank you," he took his crossbow and began to leave.

Anastasia Sikorsky smiled.

Gorski was up early and at the gymnasium, running in place on one of the several treadmills. Gorski had finished twelve laps, the equivalent of four miles, when his communication device attached to his right wrist began to vibrate. He looked at the written message on the screen as he kept running. It was an order from Captain Sowa for Gorski to report to the lower Docking Bay where the Super Raumschiffs were resting. Gorski stopped running, stepped off of the machine, and walked toward the gymnasium exit. Something was up. The tone of Captain's message seemed intentionally vague regarding the reason for the meeting.

Gorski walked quickly to the stair case and descended several flights to the level of the vessel where the junior officer quarters were located. He rushed to his private quarters and placed his palm on the security check at his doorway. The computer scanned his hand and confirmed that his identity and the doors slid open for him. Gorski began pulling off his workout clothes as he walked toward his shower. He did not want to be late for his second mission as a MI officer. His father had taught him that the military expected promptness. The tardy soldiers were the ones that would be passed over for promotion. He wanted to advance in rank and in position. Making a good impression on the higher ranking officers was important to him.

As he showered, Gorski thought of how fortunate he was. He had communicated with his younger brother, Piotr, late last night. Gorski learned through Piotr that there had been an attack at the ballroom during Golden Harvard's celebration. He was relieved that his brother and father were not harmed, other than having been stunned. But the murder of Lupita Calderon was senseless to him. She had never harmed anyone and she kept a low profile at the Academy. She came from a large family and had numerous siblings. The only times Lupita seemed to call attention to herself was when she helped chase the Ragnarsson space ship named *Blitzkrieg* and when she recently testified against the Ragnarsson's at the media event trial against the conspirators. Gorski leaned against the shower wall as the warm water soothed his skin. The Ragnarsson's were the only ones that would have any anger towards Lupita. He concluded that her murder had to be the work of one of those assassins. The only question in his mind that he could not answer was why they would kidnap Dirk and Therese.

Gorski quickly dried off and dressed in his solid black Class C uniform. He checked his weaponry on his web belt and began to move for the door. He hoped that wherever Dirk and Therese were, they were safe. He slid his feet into his over the ankle combat boots and tightened them with the Velcro fasteners. He ran out the door to make roll call in the docking bay. He wanted to make a good impression by being one of the first officers to arrive.

Unfortunately for Gorski, he was not the first member of the two search and rescue teams to respond. When Gorski arrived, he saw that Space Command and

Search and Rescue Lieutenant Hans Streicher was already present, taking inventory of boxes of supplies at the floor next to Super Raumschiff *Cortez 14*. He was wearing his dark blue Class C uniform which had a red stripe on the sleeves, just above the wrist, which signified that he was also a member of the elite search and rescue division. Gorski recalled that his friends Mary Lincoln and Alan Anderson took the additional training to qualify as members of search and rescue. They had related to Gorski that the course was difficult. Next to Streicher was Captain Mara Sowa, directing some repair technicians on which search function robots were needed to be loaded on board the Raumschiff's for the mission. Sowa was in her solid black Class C outfit, her hair pulled up with pins.

The second Super Raumschiff, *Cortez 7*, also had some activity. Gorski observed Lieutenant Vela in her dark blue Class C uniform taking inventory, just as Streicher was at the other ship. Lieutenant Jim Shigeta, dressed in his black Class C uniform, was assisting the pilot.

Gorski walked straight towards Captain Sowa and saluted her. "Lieutenant Gorski reporting for duty, ma'am."

Sowa and Streicher returned the salute, Streicher out ranked Gorski as well.

"Good morning, Yuri." Sowa smiled at him. "You

are assigned to Cortez 7 with Shigeta and Vela. Why don't you give them a hand in loading the search robots and the supplies?"

"This is an actual mission?" Gorski concluded.

"Correct, Lieutenant. I believe it will be your second real action since coming on board the Cortez." Sowa observed. "After the way you handled yourself on the Blood Moon, this will be a piece of cake for you."

"What is the mission, ma'am?"

"We are going to board and search two derelict Battle Cruisers," Sowa told him. She noticed a hint of Gorski's eyes widening with interest. Sowa concluded that the young officer probably had a split second flashback of how his mother died, on a mission to a derelict ship. "Go join Shigeta and Vela. Try not to get injured this time."

"Yes ma'am," Gorski turned and walked over to the other Raumschiff. He saluted Shigeta and Vela, both of whom outranked him. Salutes were returned.

Shigeta motioned for Gorski to help him carry in the plastic boxes of supplies. Gorski picked up one box by the handle bars on the side; he realized it must weigh about seventy-five pounds. He followed Shigeta up the back entrance ramp of the transport ship. Shigeta set down his supply box and began fastening it to some of the safety cables to ensure the box would not shift during flight. Gorski did the same with his.

When the two men finished and walked back down the ramp to the docking bay platform. Gorski noticed that Harrison, Dominic and engineering Lieutenant Danica Garcia were present, assisting the others. It took less than an hour to stock both of the Raumschiff's with supplies and weapons. Once the job was completed. Captain Sowa ordered the group to huddle close together at parade rest.

Gorski noted that there were two platoons of Marines, sixteen nurses, two medical doctors: Laurent Sowa and Erik Macinlock, eight engineers, twenty-five different types of fully functional mechanical robots, Brennan and Malveaux. There were a few MI enlisted personnel, Lewis among them. Gorski saw that Command Sergeant Major Kay Jordan Light was organizing the two platoons of Marines. Light was a big man, almost seven feet tall and as muscular as Harrison. He was over fifty years old, far past the time of retiring from military service. But Light loved his work too much and refused to go off to tend a farm or write his memoirs.

One of the engineering officers caught Gorski's attention. She was a strikingly beautiful Child of Athena. Her snow white skin gave her away. But her hair was not dark like the other Harcourt's Gorski had met in the past. The same was true for her eye color, it was different. This woman was blonde with blue eyes. She must have sensed that Gorski was staring at her as she slowly turned her head in his direction and their eyes met. She smiled at him and he smiled back. He wondered why he had never seen her before on the Battle Cruiser. She was never at Take Ten, never at the gymnasium or firing range when Gorski was there. He speculated that the woman worked different shift times than he had. Gorski determined that he wanted to get to know her after the meeting was disbanded.

"Ladies and gentlemen," Captain Sowa greeted them while pacing in front of the assembled group. "You all have top secret clearances. What I tell you now may not be repeated to anyone. We have located two of the ships from the Eighth Fleet. Long range telescopic photographs reveal one of the ships to be the Flag Ship, the *Cleopatra.* Our scientists have concluded the second is the *Tonkin Gulf.* Scans indicate no life forms are on the vessels. That means either there are fifteen hundred dead on board each ship or the crew has gone missing.

"We also have picked up fourteen of the eighteen Transport ships that were being escorted to Planet Cootron by the Fleet. Similarly, all fourteen transports have no life forms on board. We have scanned for communication beacons from the Fleet, in hopes that Admiral Cardenas or his crew sent out some warning or information regarding the events that led to the fate of the ships and the crew. We have found nothing. How this occurred is a complete mystery."

Sowa paused and stopped in front of Gorski and Dominic, who were standing next to Harrison. "You two were six year old boys on the Argonaut when a search and rescue mission went very badly. Gorski, your mother was one of the Marines that died on the derelict ship she boarded."

Dominic swallowed hard. He was one of the children at the day care that had consoled Gorski when his mother had died. It was how they met and subsequently grew into lifelong friends. He knew the mention of the death of his mother was painful to Gorski still, even after the passage of the years. Gorski hid his emotions well, showing no reaction to Sowa's words.

"Because of that tragedy from the Argonaut event, the protocol has changed when we attempt to board an abandoned vessel." Sowa continued walking again. "We will board each of the Battle Cruisers if, and only if, our service robots clear it. These robots go in first and scan the lower levels and work their way up. Understood?"

The Marines present shouted out the others with a "Ma'am yes ma'am!"

"Good," Sowa continued. "Once the lower levels are cleared, we will secure the Docking Bay of each Battle Cruiser and then work our way to the next major level which contains the engine rooms and life supports systems. Our experts here will try and power the vessels back up and make repairs. While on the Battle Cruiser's you are all ordered to keep your enviro-suits on at all times until the mission commander, which is me, orders that it is safe to remove the suits. I want all of you armed to the teeth. On each ship are enough hand lasers, laser rifles, flame throwers, knives, stun darts, flame darts and other weaponry for your use. Do not be shy. Hopefully we will have no need for offensive capability. But if we do, better to have it on you than wish you had."

"Better to be judged by twelve than carried by six?" Doctor Erik Macinlock joked.

Several of the civilians present laughed. The military portion of the group kept straight faces.

Captain Sowa paused for a few seconds to allow the laughter to subside. "We meet back here in exactly twenty-four hours. I expect each of you to be in uniform, in enviro-suits and ready to proceed. Get plenty of rest; it may be quite some time before you sleep again. Dismissed!"

The crowd began to disperse. Gorski watched as Captain Sowa and her husband, Doctor Sowa began walking toward the metal staircase to leave the floor of the Docking Bay. Gorski received a quick hug from his friend Dominic as he was trying to find the Harcourt woman he had met eyes with earlier. She was nowhere in sight.

"What is wrong, my friend?" Dominic was looking in the direction that Gorski was.

"I was looking for someone," Gorski shrugged. "Care for a bite to eat at Take Ten?"

"I am starving," Dominic answered. "Drew?"

Harrison nodded in agreement, "Yes, let's go eat. Hey, did any of you two see that Harcourt woman with the engineers?"

"Didn't notice," Gorski wanted to stay off the subject. Although Murdock had proven to be a great lover, the sight of the Harcourt woman moved Gorski somehow. He had known female Children of Athena from his days at the Clovis Academy. There had been Ann Harcourt, who Gorski recalled as a decent lady. Then there was Melissa Harcourt who was a schemer and an intentional home wrecker. The two had been polar opposites in their approach to friends and interacting with others. Melissa had been known to use her genetically enhanced powers to her benefit while Ann had never used them. Gorski had also had as one of his closest friends a male Harcourt named Jack. He had been more like Ann, refusing to use his powers of causing others to become sexually aroused, or controlling their thoughts or reading their minds. Gorski wondered what this mystery Harcourt woman aboard the *Cortez* was like.

Gorski followed Harrison and Dominic up the long ramp toward the metal staircase. The three men ascended them rapidly. Food was awaiting them.

The three men found that Take Ten was not very busy and located a round table to relax in quite easily.   The robot waiter took their orders and left. Soon, hot coffee, cranberry juice and water was delivered to them.

Dominic poured a shot of cream into his coffee. "Did you both hear about Lupita?"

Gorski nodded.

Harrison frowned, "You mean Lupita Calderon? The pilot candidate back at Clovis Academy?"

"She was murdered," Gorski told Harrison.

Harrison sat back in his chair, trying his best to picture the face of Lupita in his mind. He had barely said two words to Calderon in the time she was a fellow student at the Academy. Harrison had not been in the pilot program, so the chances of spending quality time with a fellow student that was not in the same degree plan was slim. Especially since the Clovis Academy had over fourteen thousand students. Harrison only recalled that the Calderon girl had been well liked and she seemed to show heroism when it was called for. "Did they catch who did it?"

"Not that I am aware of," Dominic said and then drank some of his cranberry juice. "My brother knew her fairly well. She was in his flight battalion at the Academy. He always had good things to say about her."

"I think I know who did it," Gorski smiled as the robot waiter delivered their breakfast combination plates of eggs, French toast, poggie bacon, banana slices, blueberries and strawberries.

"You gonna keep us in suspense?" Harrison began coating his scrambled eggs with pepper. "Who killed her?"

"I think it was a Ragnarsson." Gorski finished his first cup of coffee. He motioned to the robot waiter that he needed a refill.

"And how did you come to that conclusion?" Harrison began eating one of his bacon slices.

"By deductive reasoning. She was never in any of the campus gangs. We all know her sister and brothers were with the Bragg Gang. But Lupita never joined their ranks. She never did anything bad to anyone else. The only two times she came out of her shell, so to speak, was when she tried to help bring down the Blitzkrieg and when she testified against the Ragnarsson's at the trial. The common denominator is that she stood up against those killers twice. I think they killed her to send a message."

"Not buying it man," Harrison said. "They were all dead or locked up. What about the Rosenburg's? She damaged them just as much."

"My father arrested all of the wanted Rosenburg's." Gorski told them.

"What about the ones under the radar?" Dominic said as he scooped up a spoon full of strawberries. "I mean for both families. John Rosenburg and all of his children and grandchildren were never arrested. You think he is going to take his brother being burned alive by Les Gillis' traps on the Blood Moon? And you two killing his nephews? Julia killing the other? What about the Doctor named Matthew?   They never found him. And then there were Dell Junior's widows. They all escaped capture after killing a group of MI soldiers. And we have no clue how many children Dell Junior had. What about the assassins that died during the dust storm incident? Did anyone ever investigate how many children Prescott or Chang had? What about the man that was named Montrose? Did he have any family or friends that might want to avenge him? It could be any one of them. You two really should be watching your backs more. I have warned Marco many times, you mess with family, especially a family that is close in every way, they will come after you."

"Relax, Dominic. You worry too much about things that might not even be true." Harrison laughed. "Sometimes you are way too paranoid. Who would get near us here on a Battle Cruiser? This ship is the safest place in the Universe."

"That is where you are wrong," a female voice from behind the table told them.

The three men turned around and saw the female Harcourt in her engineering uniform standing behind them. She had a nice smile and the uniform fit her well, showing off her slender curves. Gorski and his friends stood up instinctively.

"Hi, I am..." Gorski began before the Harcourt

woman cut him off.

"You are Yuri Gorski?" She shook his hand. She walked over to Harrison and Dominic and shook theirs as well. "Drew Harrison and Dominic Andolini. Everyone on this ship knows who you three are." Jan Eis Harcourt, like the rest of the population, had seen the Blood Moon Incident play out live, thanks to the satellite broadcasts. When the crew of the *Cortez* learned that two of the heroes of that event, Gorski and Harrison, were selected to serve with them, it had raised morale. They were media stars, famous and proved themselves as men willing to fight against odds most men would have run from.

"And your name?" Gorski asked.

"I am Lieutenant Jan Eis Harcourt and work in the Engineering section," she introduced herself. "Are all of the seats taken? May I join you?"

"Please do join us," Gorski walked over to one of the empty chairs and pulled it out for her. He watched as the slender woman sat down in the seat. She was smiling at him.

"So, Janice, where did you go to study engineering?" Harrison asked. He noted that she was far more beautiful than the two Harcourt women back at Clovis Academy. Melissa had been shorter and had an evil disposition about her. Ann was cute, attractive, but not as stunning as Jan Eis.

"I studied on Sikorsky's Planet," she waved to the robot waiters in the corner so she could place her order. "I have two engineering degrees, one in mechanical engineering and my doctorate was in hydraulic engineering. And my name is two words, not Janice, but Jan Eis. The people that raised me were Germanic and called me Eis, or the English word for ice, due to my snow white skin. You can imagine that all of us that were Harcourt's startled our birth parents greatly when they saw the color of our skin."

"So, may we call you Jan?" Gorski inquired as the robot waiter arrived. He waited as the Harcourt woman gave her order.

"You, Yuri Gorski, may call me whatever you wish if you are able to get me behind closed doors." She was smiling at him as she spoke.

Harrison and Dominic gave each other a look, both deciding to finish their food quickly so that their friend could get to know the lady.

Jan Eis looked at Dominic and Harrison. "Do not eat so quickly gentlemen. I am not interested in only one man. I want to learn about each of you."

"You were reading our minds?" Harrison asked

defensively.

"No, I did not have too. Your body language said it all." Jan Eis smiled at the robot waiter as it delivered her coffee and water. "I am one of the more advanced second generation Harcourts. I sense things without even trying. Mr. Harrison, you said this ship is the safest place in the Universe. You are wrong. I see things; sometimes I can see the future. I have seen death coming to this ship. I see it in my dreams. Soon, we will all be in the middle of a war. Many will die. I have never seen visions like this before. So, this ship is not safe."

"You have had dreams before, about the future?" Dominic felt a chill go down his spine as he recalled that Jack Harcourt had once told him that he would have dreams that would come true. The woman sounded confident in her predictions.

"My dreams always come true," Jan Eis told them. "I cannot tell you why we will be fighting, or against who. But I have seen a fleet of superior ships, in sizes and shapes I have never been exposed to, that will cause much havoc to the rest of us. I have heard the screams of the dying. I cannot stop the dreams from coming. With each passing night, the visions grow stronger." Being a Harcourt or a Child of Athena can be a curse, she thought to herself. She began to wonder if it had been wise to tell these men about her ability to see into the future. She could never control the focus of her ability. The visions always came to her in her sleep and they were always random events.

"So, what should we do to prepare ourselves?" Gorski asked.

"We should live life to its' fullest," Jan Eis laughed, trying to lighten the mood. "So, tell me gentlemen, what kind of woman turns your heads? Dominic has a wedding ring on, so he is spoken for. That is, unless you are looking for more wives? Yuri, Drew, which of you two would be amenable to having a Harcourt woman in your life?"

"I am kind of involved," Harrison admitted. "But you make me wish I wasn't."

Everyone began laughing at that.

"So, Yuri Gorski, are you available?" Jan Eis asked.

"Well I am seeing someone right now," he told her.

Harcourt frowned, "Laura Murdock?"

Gorski sat back in his chair and stared at her for a few seconds before asking her: "Are you reading my mind?"

"No, I am not. I just happen to be in on all of the

gossip on the ship." She drank some of her water. "It is all over the gossip that you are her next heart break."

"Heartbreak? What do you mean by that?" Gorski stopped cutting his French toast and set his utensils on the table.

"I suppose that no one has told you three boys that Laura is not a woman to be trusted," Jan Eis whispered to them.

"Why are you whispering?" Dominic wanted to know.

"Because the three of you are Narcs. Militzia. Polizei. That would account for why you have not been included in the ship's gossip."

"Narcs?" Harrison demanded as he gave one of his famous frowns. "Who would call us that?"

"Everyone on the ship," Jan Eis pointed her fork at their uniforms. "You are all wearing black. That is the MI color. That makes you three Narcs. No one will confide in you out of fear that you will get them into trouble. Every one worries that they may say something out of context and the soldiers in black will make them disappear. Didn't you boys know that before you volunteered for MI?"

"No, we didn't." Gorski grunted, thinking he should have stayed with his original major, the pilot corps with the Space Command. "So, why can't I trust Murdock?"

"She uses men," Jan Eis shrugged. "You are one of many that she has seduced. You won't be the last. Just watch your back, Yuri Gorski. You seem like a good person. I would hate to see you get burned by that Jezebel."

"I'll be careful," Gorski assured her.

"Doesn't matter. She will find a way to hurt you," Jan Eis promised.

Gorski watched as the robot waiter delivered a plate of crab meat egg salad for Jan Eis. Gorski recalled his friend at the Academy, Jack Harcourt, used to eat mostly meals with eggs in them. He had told Gorski that all of the Harcourt's craved eggs. Scrambled, over-easy, hard boiled or mixed with other foods such as the crab salad Jan Eis was now eating. Gorski caught her smiling at him as she ate a bite of her meal. She swallowed and licked her full lips and smiled at him.

Doctor Erik Macinlock returned to his spacious quarters on the second Level of the Battle Cruiser. Since he was a medical doctor and a high ranking civilian employee, his room was twice the size as the ones assigned to Gorski, Dominic and Harrison. Only the doctorate employees and high ranking officers were given what were known as the Executive Suites. Macinlock began packing a large suitcase for the mission to the listing battle cruisers. He planned on taking enough clothing, soap, toothpaste and toiletries to last a minimum of one week. There was no way to be certain how long the mission would take.

He turned his head as his sliding doors at the entrance opened. Laura Murdock walked in with a smile on her face. She was wearing a long black coat that went from her neck to her ankles. She was barefoot.

"Laura," Macinlock sighed when he realized who it was. He had forgotten to reprogram his entrance security. He had meant to eliminate her palm print access to his room after she had broken off their relationship. He watched in silence as Murdock removed her black coat to reveal she was naked underneath. Macinlock had not been involved with another woman since Murdock had ended their short lived sexual relationship. Thus, he was ripe for seduction.

Murdock moved to him and wrapped her arms around Macinlock's neck and began kissing him passionately. She pressed her curvaceous body against him. He responded by kissing her lips and neck.

As she allowed Macinlock to make love to her,

Murdock mused that seducing the doctor was too easy. It was like bribing a dog with a biscuit. After he climaxed, the doctor fell asleep, as he always did after sex with Murdock. She slid out of his bed and walked to her coat and pulled out two microchips, just like the one that Anastasia Sikorsky had planted on Dominic's crossbow. Murdock affixed one of the microchips on Macinlock's luggage. She taped the second on his medical uniform that was on one of his chairs. After she was done, Murdock put the coat back on and left the snoring doctor behind.

Murdock had to go to her quarters and shower to cover up her little rendezvous with the doctor. She enjoyed how simple it was to manipulate men. She had found that if she showed a little cleavage, smiled the right way, men would jump off of a cliff for her. Murdock now needed to divide and conquer. Murdock had told Anastasia Sikorsky that Gorski, Harrison and Dominic were like the Three Musketeers. They were always together, good friends, loyal to one another and had shown they would stand by each other no matter what. She had tried to seduce Dominic and failed. He was one of those rare men that would probably love only one woman for life. Murdock concluded that Dominic was a fool to turn away the opportunity to enjoy her companionship. Gorski was easy because he had so much lust built up for her. Now she wanted to test Harrison. If she could break up Harrison with the annoying enlisted girl Lewis and fracture his friendship with Gorski, then that success would make Murdock's day. And, it would hopefully cause enough friction that would end the Gorski and Harrison friendship forever.

After finishing breakfast, Harrison and Dominic returned to their quarters. They had been instructed by Captain Sowa to get plenty of rest, and that was what they both intended to do. Harrison was in his own quarters for all of fifteen minutes when he heard his security bell ring, signifying someone was at his door.

"Come in!" Harrison bellowed. If it was LaShondra Lewis, she would have just walked on in as she was cleared by Harrison to have access to his room.

He was puzzled when he saw that it was Laura Murdock at his door. She walked in slowly, smiling broadly. "So Mister Harrison, where is little Miss Lewis hiding?"

Harrison stood to his feet. He watched as the desirable woman approached him. Murdock was wearing a skin tight tube top and shorts. She was barefoot. Harrison took in a deep breath. He was fighting the urge to grab her in his arms and take her.

"Um, she is on duty." Harrison answered slowly. "Is there something I can help you with? Weren't you going to meet up with Yuri?"

Murdock stopped about three feet from Harrison. "Yes, you can help me and no I wasn't going to meet Yuri."

"What can I do for you?" Harrison was almost afraid to ask.

Murdock reached down with both of her hands and pulled her tube top off, revealing her bare breasts to Harrison. She watched his eyes to see the reaction Harrison had to her undressing. She could tell that he liked what he saw. She moved in on him, not giving him a chance to say anything honorable. She began running her hands all over his body, standing up on her toes to kiss him. Harrison found the woman so desirable that he decided to have sex with her. They were on the floor, Murdock unzipping Harrison's Class C uniform. His hands were running over her body. Murdock relaxed and let Harrison take her. Enjoy your work, Murdock told herself.

Jake Brown had been trained to be a good leader of men and women. One of the leadership qualities he had been taught was to make certain his Marines kept regular physical examinations and mental health evaluations. Over the past century the experts in the psychiatric community had conducted studies on several cases in which humans ended up in psychiatric wards due to spending too much time in outer space. Brown believed that he had to set the example for the Marines under his command. So, when he was summoned by Doctor Laurent Sowa to the medical section of the space craft for an evaluation, Brown reported to demonstrate to his platoon that it was critical to follow medical directives. Brown had recently undergone a physical evaluation and hoped that the doctor was going to give him a clean bill of health. Brown was a bit concerned that the results had taken one week to arrive.

Brown entered the lobby of the medical area and observed a few service men and women waiting to be seen in the rows of seats. The Lieutenant checked in with the computer screen to report that he was present as requested by the doctor. Before Brown could sit down he heard his voice called out. He turned around and saw Doctor Sowa standing in the doorway to his left.

"Lieutenant, this way please," Sowa instructed him.

Brown, the dutiful soldier, walked straight toward the doctor and through the open doorway. He did not see that Anastasia Sikorsky was hiding behind the opened door. As Brown followed Sowa down the narrow hallway,

Anastasia crept up behind him and stabbed a stun dart into the muscular officer's neck. Brown collapsed to the ground and found that he was unable to move. He heard Sowa whistle and five Marine Corps enlisted men walked down from the opposite end the hallway toward Brown. Anastasia had assisted Sowa with this form of ambush several times before.

"Get the Lieutenant in the operating room," Sowa instructed. "We have less than an hour before the mission."

"Yes, Doctor." One of the Private's answered.

Brown felt himself being lifted into the air by the five Marines. They carried him into an operating room where a nurse was waiting for him. Brown was carefully placed on an operating table face down. He felt the nurse inject a needle into his left arm.

Doctor Sowa walked into the room and stood next to Brown's prone figure. "Do not be frightened, Lieutenant. You will not die. I am going to perform a little operation on you. When you wake up in the morning, it will be as if it had never happened. But you will be under my command. Nurse Rendon, have you administered the sedatives?"

"Yes Doctor," she answered.

"Good. Scalpel." Sowa instructed.

Brown felt no pain as Doctor Sowa used a saw to

cut open his skull. The Doctor skillfully placed into Brown's brain a microchip which would enable the doctor to override Brown's free will. Sowa had already done the same procedure to his wife, Captain Mara Sowa and to two squads of Marines. Sowa planned on conducting the same medical procedure on each and every non-Royal Family member on board. Within the month, Sowa planned on having at least a platoon of Marines under his control as well as a few more ranking officers.

Harrison was groggy when he woke up to find himself naked on his bed. He was surprised to find that he was not alone. Murdock was lying on his chest, naked as well. She smiled at him and kissed him on the lips. Harrison felt as if he had been drugged.

"What time is it?" Harrison mumbled. He vaguely remembered having sex with Murdock. But he could not recall falling asleep with her.

Before Murdock could answer, the doors to Harrison's quarters slid open. LaShondra Lewis walked into the room. "Hey baby! How was your...."

Lewis froze stiff when she saw the man she loved lying naked with the Murdock woman. Lewis at first did not want to believe the scene before her, shaking her head left to right. Tears began to form in her eyes, her heart pounding with pain due to the betrayal she stumbled upon.

Harrison jumped to his feet, pushing Murdock aside. "Honey! Wait. I can explain!"

"Fuck you!" Lewis screamed as she stormed out of his quarters. She was running down the hallway, pushing past several crewmen as she ran. She could hear Harrison pleading with her to come back. She made it to the elevator lift before the tears began to flow down her cheeks. She stepped into the lift after the doors slid open. She did not look back to see if Harrison was following her. She leaned into the back of the lift and covered her face with her hands as she wept.

Her mind was spinning and she felt as if she were going to vomit. Lewis had been a MI undercover agent on planet New Edinburgh when she met Harrison. The attraction between them had been immediate and they were inseparable. When Harrison graduated and received his commission, he joined the *Cortez* crew. To follow the man, Lewis requested and received a transfer. She left behind a great leader and a group of fellow undercover operatives that she had deeply enjoyed working with. She gave up everything to follow Harrison for his dreams of serving on a Battle Cruiser. Heart broken, she returned to her assigned sleeping area, where the enlisted men and women were housed. She walked past several Privates and Corporals to her bunk bed in the Enlisted Section. She jumped onto the top of her assigned bunk bed and wept.

Harrison watched helplessly as Lewis stormed out of his room and most certainly out of his life. He put his head down in shame then turned to see that Murdock had already dressed and she was laughing at him.

"You think this is funny?" Harrison demanded. "Do you have any idea what this means?"

Murdock continued laughing. "Of course I know what this means, she will never forgive you. I finally got to get laid by a man outside of my race, and I quite enjoyed it, thank you. But, now I must be off. Your old friend Yuri Gorski will be expecting me soon."

"You planned on this happening!" Harrison growled. "You seduced me just so you could cause this. You, you drugged me!"

"Now why would I go and do a thing like that?" Murdock was still laughing. "I just wanted to have sex with a man that was almost seven feet tall and solid muscle. I got what I wanted. And frankly, you did too. All men want me. I just gave you your best piece of ass you will ever have. You should be thanking me."

Harrison shook his head in disbelief. He wished he

could turn back time, to tell her no when she walked in his room. But the damage was done and it was irreparable. The last person in the universe that Harrison had wanted to harm was Lewis. "I should have told you no. I should have sent you away."

"But you didn't," Murdock was no longer laughing. She pushed herself past Harrison. "Face it; you enjoyed yourself and so did I. Now, you tell Yuri that I let you fuck me, I will deny it. I bet he would believe me since I will be the one pleasuring him in his bed. Don't you dare try and cross me, Drew Harrison. You will regret it."

Harrison watched helplessly as Murdock calmly walked out of his quarters. Harrison slid down to the floor and sat there for several minutes, trying to get his mind around what had happened and how it had happened. Harrison had never been in love with Lewis, not like he had been with Julia Steiner. But both relationships ended badly due to his actions. "I lost Julia because I was a drunk and now this. I am such a screw up." He put his head in his hands. He wanted to go to Lewis, to explain to her and apologize. But he knew there was no way to repair what he had done. Murdock presented herself to him and he had a choice. Harrison chose momentary pleasure over what was right. He betrayed both Lewis and Gorski at the same time.

The two people closest to him in his life and he could not take it back.

Murdock was jubilant as she reflected on her accomplishments for the past twelve hours. She had split up Lewis and Harrison and damaged Harrison's friendship with Gorski. She had drugged Harrison as they had sex together. She had done so with a sleeping medication that she had coated on her lips. When Harrison kissed her, he had sealed his fate. As Murdock made love to Harrison, he slowly lost consciousness. Murdock had spied on Harrison for weeks and knew exactly when Lewis would get off duty and show up at his quarters. The plan worked out exactly as Murdock had planned it. While Harrison was out, Murdock planted the same tracking device on his uniform as she had done to the pathetic Doctor Macinlock. She also took some digital photographs of herself naked with Harrison, to show to Yuri Gorski at the right time. She would make Gorski fall in love with her and then reveal Harrison's betrayal of his friendship.

It had been a very good day.

CHAPTER SIX

Yuri Gorski donned his Class C uniform and quickly arrived at the Super Raumschiff *Cortez 7,* about an hour before the time Captain Sowa had ordered. He had a black suitcase packed with extra undergarments, two additional Class C uniforms and toiletries. He had spent the night with Laura Murdock; the sex had been amazing as it had been the first time he was with her. Murdock was being left behind on the *Cortez* as temporary chief of security. What Gorski did not know was that Murdock had placed a tracing disc on his uniform, just as she had done to Harrison and Murdock.

Gorski was met by Jim Shigeta and pilot Paula Vela at the lower entrance to the ship. The three for them walked up the entrance ramp to find their required enviro-suits waiting. The three began to suit up.

"You were also a pilot?" Shigeta asked of Gorski, knowing the answer before he had asked the question.

Shigeta made it his business to know each and every detail of the talents of the men and women that are under his command during a mission. Shigeta had spent the last day studying the employee files of each of the team members on his Super Raumschiff. For Gorski, it was easy reading. Shigeta knew of Gorski's part in the Blood Moon Incident, which included several hours of solo piloting a Raumschiff over the lunar surface.

"Yes sir," Gorski answered as he secured his gloves to the black colored envito-suit.

"Good," Shigeta said and pointed at Vela. "You will be her co-pilot. We are assigned to the Cleopatra. When we board her, I will be the temporary Captain of that Battle Cruiser. We do not know what happened to these ships. The aggressors may still be out there somewhere. So, I need you and Paula to be ready."

Gorski nodded, "I won't let you down, sir."

"We will be ready," Vela promised as she turned her attention toward Gorski. "Well, Lieutenant? Would you care to join me in the Pilot Command module? We have engine checks to complete." Vela was happy to get the handsome Gorski alone with her. Perhaps she could gain his confidence so she could warn him of Murdock and her bad intentions.

Gorski followed Vela up the metallic stairs from the bottom storage area to the second floor of the Super Raumschiff. They walked around several winding hallways until they arrived at the Command Offices of the space craft. To their right was the computer section, the life support and weapons command. To their left was the section for the ship commander and advisors. In that section was a metal ladder that led up to the pilot module. Vela climbed up the ladder first with Gorski right behind her. She sat down in the pilot's seat and Gorski sat next to her in the co-pilot's.

"Computer, Lieutenant Vela of UNSC. Please verify my voice prints so we may begin systems check."

The computer responded that she was cleared. She began calmly checking all systems as Gorski assisted her. She smiled at Gorski after the twenty minute exercise was completed.

"So, we are clear for lift off?" Gorski smiled back.

Vela nodded to him, "Something has been bugging me about you. May I ask you a personal question?"

"Certainly."

"Why MI? Why didn't you stay with the Space Command as a pilot?"

Gorski shrugged, "MI seemed to be the way to go.

I love to fly ships. But MI seems to get all the action."

Vela laughed at that. She pointed out the see-through metallic observation window in front of both of them. "Well, let's hope that there will be little to no action out there."

"If there is any action," Gorski patted his hand on his hand laser snapped on his right hip of his enviro-suit, "I will protect you."

"Protect yourself. I can do pretty well on my own," Vela assured him and patted the hand laser hanging from her hip. "You men are ridiculous sometimes. I am not a shrinking violet in need of being rescued. If there is action waiting for us I will be right next to you, kicking ass."

Harrison had been one of the last to board the *Cortez 7*. He had been unable to sleep the night before due to his guilt over having sex with Murdock. He had tried to contact Lewis several times, but she had blocked his calls and messages. Harrison dressed in his enviro-suit, saying nothing to the others around him. He was lost in his own thoughts. He wanted to talk with Gorski, tell him what had happened before Murdock did so. He noticed that one of the engineers on board the ship was Jan Eis Harcourt. She was staring at him with sympathy. Harrison wondered if she had read his mind. He heard her voice in his head saying "Yes." Harrison glared at her, but she was already walking past the storage area and toward the engine room. He felt uneasy being around someone that could read his thoughts without his knowledge.

Shigeta did a head count on his crew. The platoon of Marines was on board as were the search and scanner robots. The engineers were ready. Shigeta walked up the stairs to the second floor of the space craft. He asked the computer to patch him into the rest of the ship. "We have been cleared to proceed to the Cleopatra. She is still floating in space, with no real direction. Command is reporting that there are still no life forms. Maintain safety at all times and all of us will come home. Lieutenant Vela, the mission is in your hands. Take us to the Cleopatra."

"Yes sir," Vela smiled.

Gorski watched as the pilot maneuvered the half circle steering mechanism upward which caused the solar and nuclear powered hybrid engine to lift the Super Raumschiff about ten feet from the docking bay floor. She then pressed a few buttons on the computer console before her and the ship began to fly forward slowly. Within two minutes, the *Cortez 7* was leaving behind the Battle Cruiser *Cortez* and entering the darkness of outer space.

"Distance to the Cleopatra?" Vela asked Gorski.

"One hundred kilometers," Gorski read from his computer screen on the astral navigation panel. "We should dock with her within thirty minutes."

Vela nodded that she understood and steered the Super Raumschiff in the direction of the Battle Cruiser. "Computer, enlarge the image of the Cleopatra."

Gorski and Vela looked at the magnified image of the Battle Cruiser. She was floating, all exterior lights were off. There were no signs of laser burns or breaches on the hull. Gorski inspected the large war ship. He wondered how a crew of over fifteen hundred could have just vanished into thin air.

Gorski chatted with Vela about several topics as she flew the Space Craft with ease. She was experienced and confident at her job. Finally, Gorski mustered up enough courage to ask her about the big pink elephant in the room.

"What can you tell me about Laura Murdock?"

Vela was silent for several seconds, staring out into space. Finally she looked at Gorski. "She is someone I consider a friend. But, then I am not a male."

"What do you mean by that?" Gorski frowned.

"She has been known to cause some trouble," Vela paused. She wanted to tell him everything. Unfortunately she was concerned that the man would not believe her words and run to Murdock and tell her all Vela told him. "I would not let her date my little brother."

"You have anything, any specific acts by Laura, to back that up?"

Vela sighed, "Go talk to Jason Allen or Doctor Macinlock. I'm certain they would be better able to tell you more about what Laura is all about. I really don't feel comfortable saying any more."

Gorski smiled. "Are you uncomfortable because I am a Narc?"

Vela began laughing, "You do wear the black uniform. Should I be scared?"

Gorski looked out the observation window and watched as the *Cleopatra* grew closer with each passing second. "I would never turn you in Lieutenant Vela."

"You may end up eating those words," Vela said as the onboard computer alerted the crew that they were a mere five kilometers from the *Cleopatra* Docking Bay.

"Decreasing speed," Gorski informed Vela.

Jan Eis was in the engineering section of the *Cortez 7* when the alert sounded to be ready for docking with the *Cleopatra*. She had assisted Jin-Woo's efforts to prepare the robotic scanners. There were thirteen of the robots that varied in height from four feet tall to eight feet tall. All of the robots moved on the floors with four parallel treads for legs, similar to those of the old World War II tanks. Each of the robots had humanoid faces, necks that were made of a metal alloy that could stretch out several feet. They also had six arms each. The robots were all painted orange. The torsos of the robot scanners were thick containing several computerized memory cells to compare each and every encountered enigma with something that mankind had faced in the past. Their purpose was to clear the Docking Bay of any dangerous organisms and locate any potential weapons that had been planted to be set off as death traps.

Jan Eis nodded to Jin-Woo as she finished the last calibrations on a biological scanning robot. They were all ready to perform their functions.

Shigeta and Harrison had taken over the computer technician section of the *Cortez 7*. The two Military Intelligence officers had been using the security codes for the Cleopatra to open the outer hull of the Battle Cruiser's Docking Bay. They both watched the three dimensional image of the *Cleopatra* Docking Bay slowly open. As the massive metallic hull slid open on the right side of the *Cleopatra*, Shigeta was able to begin scanning the inside of the vessel. What he found was astounding.

Shigeta looked at Harrison with a puzzled

expression. "The Docking Bays are empty. No drone ships, no Raumschiffs and no Fighter ships. They are all gone."

Harrison returned the look at Shigeta. "But there should be over seven hundred small fighter ships on the Cleopatra and at least fifty Raumschiff's. What happened to them?"

"Looks like they abandoned ship," Corporal Offut remarked.

As the bottom level to the *Cleopatra* opened to allow *Cortez 7* to enter, Shigeta and Harrison noted that two human bodies were sucked out into the vacuum of outer space from the Battle Cruiser.

"Computer, scan those bodies," Shigeta demanded.

"Two deceased males," The computer reported. "Neither was wearing an enviro-suit. Estimate that both were dead for several weeks."

"What happened in there?" Harrison said to himself. "Did they have to abandon ship? They must have taken the Raumschiffs and fighters and fled. But from what?"

"That is what we are going to find out," Shigeta sounded confident. He reached out with his right hand and pressed some buttons on the control panel before him and activated the flood lights for the *Cortez 7*. The powerful lights illuminated the interior of the Docking Bay of the

U.N.S.C. *Cleopatra.*

It was completely empty.

Harrison checked his hand lasers. Clearly there had been a horrible disaster on the massive Battle Cruiser named the *Cleopatra.* Harrison wished he had drunk another cup of coffee. He realized that Professor Brennan was looking over his shoulder. Harrison, like all of the crew of the *Cortez,* knew that Brennan was the wise counsel of the Captain.

"What do you make of it, Professor?" Harrison wanted to know.

Brennan grunted, "They ran away from something or to some other destination. Leaving the two Battle Cruisers behind would only make sense for two reasons."

"Which would be what?" Shigeta joined the conversation.

"One, because they had no choice. That is, there is some force on the two Battle Cruisers that Admiral Cardenas and his crew could not overcome." Brennan was stroking his chin thoughtfully as he spoke. "The second would be, perhaps they left these ships in the hopes they would be found and we, as the explorers that happened upon them first, would find the clues to lead us to them."

"How can you come to that conclusion?" Harrison

asked.

Brennan looked at the approaching empty Docking Bay, nodding his head. "Yes, they left clues. If there was some force so deadly to humans on this Battle Cruiser, Admiral Cardenas would have blown the space craft up. He would have utilized the self-destruction mechanism to kill whatever was on board. I suggest that Cardenas is still out there, somewhere, and we need to unlock the clues inside this massive vessel to locate him."

Shigeta smiled at the elderly Professor. "That's a hell of a lot of assumptions there. But, I am still not taking any chances with the lives of the people on this ship. Humans board only after the robots scan, and clear, the engine room on level four. Drew, you take the point with the Marines. Once the Docking Bay has been cleared, disperse the platoon in defensive positions so we can defend the area."

"Yes sir." Harrison stood up and retrieved his four foot long laser rifle that was resting safely on a weapons rack against the wall.

"And, Lieutenant!" Shigeta called out to Harrison. "You be careful out there. Take no unnecessary risks like you did on Niles."

Harrison nodded and left Brennan and Shigeta to

discuss their theories. Harrison descended the ramps to the lower level of the ship. When he arrived, he could see the engineers maneuvering the thirteen scanner robots into position at the back ramp. Once the ramp opened, the robots would roll down the exit ramp and onto the floor of the *Cleopatra* Docking Bay. Jin-Woo and Jan Eis seemed to have everything under control. Macinlock was present as well, donning his white colored enviro-suit, his suitcase full of medical supplies next to his feet. Macinlock was lecturing the eight nurses with him to take no chances and let the Marines do the hard work for them.

Harrison already had on his black colored enviro-suit. He found his helmet on the rows of shelves against the wall and picked it up in his left hand. He watched as the platoon of Marines did the same. He checked his energy cartridge in his laser rifle. It was full. Harrison took in a deep breath and then put his black enviro-suit helmet on, securing it to the neck of his enviro-suit. He felt the *Cortez 7* land with a thud. It was time to begin the mission.

Vela smiled at Gorski as she instructed the computer to seal the outer metal bulkheads of the *Cleopatra*. She had landed the ship like a professional. They watched their three-dimensional screens as the *Cleopatra* Docking Bay doors slid shut, causing loud clanging noise followed by the hiss of the artificial atmosphere returning. They heard the computer indicate that the atmosphere on the Docking area was being replenished. If cleared by Shigeta, then the crew could remove their enviro-suit helmets.

Jan Eis and Jin-Woo secured their orange colored helmets. The computer began giving verbal warnings that the exit ramp was descending and that the outer doors of the Raumschiff would open in ten seconds. Harrison ordered the platoon of Marines to be ready. They responded by pointing their laser rifles at the exit.

The doors of the ship slid open. The robots began rolling down the exit ramp on their large treads. Harrison watched as each robot began to emit red and yellow scanning beams that were encircling the entire Docking Bay. The robots began to report in to the computer as they were rolling on the metal flooring of the *Cleopatra*.

No life signs were detected.

"Have the robots move up the ramps to the hallways into the ship," Jin-Woo instructed the computer. "They need to start their journey up the stairs and walk ramps to get to level four."

Harrison and Macinlock watched as the machines did as instructed. They were rolling up the ramps of the

Docking Bay toward the secondary bulk heads. The Docking Bay had been declared safe after the engineering and life support scans had been completed.

"Marines, move out!" Harrison ordered and led them out onto the ramp. He was the first of the group to set first on the *Cleopatra*. He pointed for the squads to secure the upper metal floors of the Docking area, as the training manuals instructed. Snipers up on the high ground, secure the low ground to protect the doctors, engineers and technicians. The Marines moved with precision. The best shooters were running up the stair cases to the second and third floors of the Docking Bay. Once in position, the sharp shooters aimed their laser weapons at different angles, each of the soldiers keeping a sharp eye out, for the safety of the civilians.

"Docking Bay secured," Harrison reported, speaking into his black colored helmet. Each of the enviro-suit helmets had communication ability as well as many other functions. The metal, see through plate glass in front of Harrison's face protected him from the deadly space vacuum and allowed him to have one hundred eighty degree visibility. Harrison stood at the foot of the exit ramp of the ship as he watched as the engineers, technicians and medical staff descend. Their safety was paramount to

Harrison and he kept his eyes darting all around as if he expected an ambush.

By now, the scanner robots were through the secondary bulk heads and in the body of the large Battle Cruiser. Shigeta walked down the ramp of the Raumschiff and looked approvingly on the locations of the Marines. Harrison had done well in securing the massive Docking Bay. Gorski was walking behind Shigeta, protecting Brennan who was in the middle of the two men. Shigeta had ordered that Vela remain on board the Raumschiff until further notice.

"The robots are sending us images of Level Four," Jin-Woo reported as he was watching his four inch long and three inch thick hand held computer. "They found something odd. I see something; it looks like several globs of, of, something I have never seen before."

"Show us," Shigeta ordered.

Jin-Woo ordered his small computer device to magnify the images to life size and broadcast them in three dimensional clarity before the team. Soon, the image was before the others. The scanner robots were sending live video feeds of the hallways leading to the engine room. Lying in the metal hallways of Level Four were eight piles of goo with Space Command uniforms lying around them, on top of them and intertwined with the substance. The colors of the piles were flesh toned, as if from a Caucasian human. There seemed to be evidence of dried blood and what appeared to be human organs around each of the eight piles.

"Scan the items," Brennan requested.

The robots paused and began to scan the eight piles with their glowing red and yellow lights. Brennan and Macinlock read the results of the electromagnetic scans. Both men looked up from their computers and shook their heads in unison.

"What is it?" Shigeta asked.

"Bodies," Macinlock said softly. "Eight human bodies. Their bone structure is non-existent. It is as if their bones were vaporized and their flesh, internal organs, muscles, nerves, brains and blood vessels collapsed on them. They are all dead."

"A new form of weapon?" Gorski asked, hoping it was not some biological entity or a new alien that feeds on human bones.

"We need to inspect their remains before we can be certain," Brennan informed them. "The scans indicate no evidence of any alien life forms. We have to work on the theory that, as Gorski suggested, these eight dead were due to some new form of weapon."

"Everyone, listen up. We have eight dead in the halls leading to the engine room. Harrison, take the first two squads of the Marines and go first. Gorski, you bring up the rear with the third squad. The fourth squad will remain behind with the civilians until the engine room is secured." Shigeta was using a calm tone of voice to assure the others he was not in panic mode. But, deep down, Shigeta was concerned. Eight people dead in such a manner, Shigeta believed that it must have been a very painful way to die.

Harrison pointed at the two Marine Corps squads and led them up the walkway ramps toward the open secondary bulkheads. As they were moving, Jin-Woo and Jan Eis began to splice into the computer system of the Docking Bay. He began typing commands onto a small keyboard in his hand that expanded when he gave a verbal command to do so. Jin-Woo moved his fingers over the computer board as it levitated just above his mid-level. His efforts were successful as he was able to restore power, causing the internal lights of the *Cleopatra* Docking Bay to come alive. The entire fifth level of the *Cleopatra* was flooded with artificial lighting.

As Harrison led the two squads of Marines into the hallway, he could hear Jin-Woo announcing that the engine room was secure. No signs of any dangerous biological or alien life forms were detected by the scanner robots. Harrison walked rapidly and found the first of the stairwells leading up to level four. Using elevator lifts on a derelict ship was against protocol, so the stairs and ladders would be the only methods to ascend and take the engine room. Harrison, without hesitation, led the Marines upward. Even though an average man might be filled with fear of what may lie around the corner, Harrison felt calm, almost serene, as he moved forward. He wondered how the other mission was faring on the U.N.S.C. *Tonkin Gulf,* hoping that Dominic and Lewis were safe.

Dominic had been ordered by Captain Sowa to take the point and lead a squad of Marines upwards to the Fourth Level where the Engine Room and Atmosphere Support Systems of the *Tonkin Gulf* were located. One of the squad members with him was LaShondra Lewis. Both Dominic and Lewis were wearing protective enviro-suits that were solid black in color with orange web belts around their midsections holding various tools and weapons in place. The Marines that accompanied them were wearing enviro-suits that were multi-colored with greens, brown and beige patterns. Their entry onto the Battle Cruiser had been similar to Gorski and Harrison's. Like the other mission, they found several dead bodies, their bone structures obliterated by some unknown force.

Dominic, with a laser pistol in one hand and a life signs scanner in the other, led his squad toward the engine room. Lewis was on his heels, her laser rifle at the ready. Dominic stepped over one of the piles of human remains; the deceased had to have been in the medical section of the *Tonkin Gulf*, the white uniform was mangled in the folds of flesh and internal organs on the floor. Lewis likewise avoided stepping on the remains, noting that it seemed as if some of the internal organs had been vomited out of the mouth of the corpse. Dominic spied upon the entrance to the engine room. There was another dead, boneless body lying at the entrance, an engineer by the color of the uniform.

Dominic placed his life signs scanner back into his utility belt and pulled out his second hand laser, holding one in each hand as his eyes were darting in several directions. There were several hallways leading to the engine room entrance. He motioned for two Marines to post themselves at the north hall, two on the east and two on the west which left himself, Lewis and five others to enter the giant engine room.

Dominic took in a deep breath and moved slowly into the engineering section. The lights had already been activated by the scanner robots. Dominic felt relieved that he could not see any other piles of human flesh on the floor. The forty foot tall nuclear-solar powered hybrid engine that powered the massive Battle Cruiser was in the far south-east corner of the engine room. The main area was open, with ceilings up to seventy-five feet high. Computers adorned the walls of the room from floor to ceiling. There were five balconies circling the upper portions of the walls. There were empty seats on the lower level, and others on the second, third, fourth and fifth balconies.

"Sir, I think I see something." Dominic heard one of the Marine Corps Privates out on the north hallway say. Dominic had posted the two men at that location to keep guard while they searched the engine room.

"I'm on my way," Dominic responded. "LaShondra, stay here and secure the engine room." He did not wait for her to respond as he darted out the engine room entrance.

Dominic ran out into the hall and was just in time to

see a stranger in a black outfit charging down the north hallway. The person had a strange white colored weapon in his hands, shaped similarly to the military issued laser rifles, but the barrel was larger in radius and it seemed just an inch wider at the stock. The stranger in black fired the weapon, releasing a kaleidoscope of colors in a beam that hit the first marine in the north hallway. The colorful beams enveloped the Marine and Dominic watched helplessly as the man was lifted off the ground, as if he were levitating. Dominic ran toward the two marines and could see the marine in the grips of the beam struggling, his enviro-suit beginning to fall into pieces on the floor. The marine screamed in a way Dominic had never heard before. The stranger fired again, the multi-colored beam hitting the second marine, who was also lifted into the air and let out a blood curdling shout that would wake the dead. Dominic watched in horror as the second Marine staggered, screaming as her body seemed to collapse upon itself. Both marines continued to scream as their bones began to dissolve into liquid. Their flesh buckled and slowly went limp, as if there were no bones inside the skin, and fell to the floor in a pile flesh.

The stranger saw Dominic and began running toward him, aiming his strange weapon. Dominic noticed that the man was wearing a Class C black Military Intelligence uniform. He was a Space Command officer. Dominic charged at the man, angered at the deaths of his two marines. At the opposite end of the hallway, Dominic observed that five more MI soldiers had rounded the corner, carrying similar weapons as the first stranger.

Dominic dived and slid to the metal floor of the hallway as the first stranger fired a blast of his unusual weapon. Dominic heard the sound of the multi-colored beam. He compared it to the popping noise bacon would normally make when being fried in a pan. The shot missed, sailing over his head and backside. He aimed his two hand lasers at the stranger. The man was running rapidly at the Italian, taking aim for another shot. Dominic fired his laser pistol in his right hand and scored a direct hit on the attacker. Dominic felt relieved when the man flipped backwards and landed on the floor with a thud.

The other five strangers seemed undeterred by the sight of the first man collapsing to the floor. They were all aiming their weapons in Dominic's direction. He began rolling on the metal floor to his right, firing both of his hand lasers at the five opponents. Dominic's accurate shooting dropped them, one by one. All five went down without getting off a shot.

Dominic was back on his feet and running toward the first man that had been wielding the strange weapon. He kicked the weapon aside and checked the man. He was a Commander, a security officer, from the *Tonkin Gulf*. His name tag read "Goodman."

Dominic ran to the first of his two marines. The weapon had been the one that caused a persons' bones to vaporize. The Marine was a pile of flesh and internal organs inside of his torn and burned enviro-suit. Dominic could not make out the identity of the dead Marine; his face was turned to mangled flesh.

Dominic turned his head in disgust. He had been warned in his days as a cadet that losing a man under your command was hard to take. Dominic lost two soldiers in a split second. He was angry at himself for not anticipating an attack. He was angrier at the unconscious Commander that had killed them.

"Lewis!" Dominic bellowed.

Lewis charged out of the engine room, her laser rifle in her hands. She saw the two piles of enviro-suits in the north hall way and Dominic picking up a strange white weapon.

"What happened?" Lewis was next to him in seconds, her eyes wide as she viewed the scene.

"We lost two Marines. This Commander was their killer; his name tag reads 'Goodman'. He must have been chief of security on this ship." Dominic surmised by the color of his clothing. They had scanned for life forms and found none. How was it that a human, a crew member of the Tonkin Gulf, and five others, could not be detected?

Dominic watched as Lewis put shackles on Commander Goodman's legs and arms and began searching him for further weapons. Dominic stepped past Lewis and made his way to the other five men that he had stunned. He frisked the first man and removed a hand laser on his belt.

Dominic sighed in disgust. "Captain Sowa, this is Lieutenant Andolini. We are not alone. A Commander Goodman and five other men attacked us without provocation. They were using weapons that I have never seen before, which I believe are the source of the bone crushing weapon. We lost two Marines in the attack. For some reason our scans for life forms did not detect these men."

Sowa, who was waiting with the rest of the mission crew of Super Raumschiff *Cortez 14* on the Docking Bay, received Dominic's transmission. She turned to her husband, Doctor Sowa and Professor Malveaux and glared at them. "Seems our technology is fallible, gentlemen. Our scanning instruments did not detect a Commander Goodman and five other crew. We have two dead Marines. Care to enlighten me as to how this could have happened?"

Malveaux did not appreciate Captain Sowa's tone of voice, but understood her anger. Two men dying were unacceptable to her. "There could be some new addition to the Cloak's of Concealment that was created by the Rosenburg Corporation a few years ago. Perhaps they can also cover up body heat, heart beats, DNA and other factors that our scanners are programmed to search for."

Sowa looked to her husband for answers. "Laurent? Any theories?"

Laurent Sowa shook his head in the negative. He was already contemplating the ramifications of the current events. The Goodman name was associated with the Sikorsky genealogy. Sowa knew of the ability to cloak one's life signs and he was well versed in the form of weapon being used. Both were derived from stolen alien technology from the Danaraja race. The Sikorsky's had kept the items secret from the rest of humanity, to be used only if an insurrection against the Royal Family began. The fact that Goodman felt the need to use the Cloak and the weapon named the bone crusher meant that the Royal Family on the *Tonkin Gulf* and *Cleopatra* had been threatened by something. Laurent Sowa, as a loyal member of the Sikorsky family, concluded that he could be in danger as well.

Captain Sowa walked over to Light, who was directing the final three squads of Marines. "Sergeant Major!"

"Yes, Captain?" Light stood at attention.

"Take a squad of marines and escort Lieutenant Danica Garcia and her other three engineers to Level Four. I need this ship operational within the hour."

Light nodded, "Yes ma'am!"

Harrison arrived at the *Cleopatra* Engine Room entrance without incident. He posted men as sentries in each hallway, just as Dominic had done on the *Tonkin Gulf.*

"Look alive Marines!" Harrison ordered as he entered the engine room. He motioned for two Marines to check the upper levels. Harrison stood before the massive hybrid engine of the *Cleopatra*. He felt a hand slap him on the back. It was Gorski.

"Drew, let's get ready. We have to get to the atmosphere controls and make sure that the ship has breathable oxygen." Gorski had his laser rifle pointed down at the floor with his index finger just outside of the trigger to avoid accidentally firing the weapon. "Dominic was attacked on the *Tonkin Gulf.*"

Harrison nodded, following Gorski back to the hall way. "I heard. Thank the stars he was not hurt." Harrison was also grateful that Lewis had not been harmed. The two men led five Marines toward the atmosphere control section which was north of the engine room. Gorski was aiming his laser rifle down the hall, ready to blast anything that came at him. After he heard the news of the undetected crew members on the *Tonkin Gulf* attacking Dominic's squad, Gorski was not willing to take any chances.

The atmosphere control room was not as large as the engine room, but it was large enough to take up twenty thousand square feet for machinery, computers and high technology oxygen conversion tanks. Scientists had been able to take the photosynthesis process and recreate it to create oxygen and enable mankind to travel in massive space craft for long distances.

Gorski pulled out a small hand held computer scanner from his left leg pouch of his enviro-suit. He ordered the small device to determine whether the conversion tanks were operable and to alert for any hidden weaponry or traps. A wide bright blue beam emanated from Gorski's electronic scanner and began running up and down each of the oxygen conversion tanks. Gorski kept up the process with each of the large machines, stepping to his right as he moved further into the room. He saw from the corner of his left eye as Jan Eis Harcourt walked in and sat down at one of the swivel chairs facing the computer desks.

"Any booby traps to be concerned with?" Jan Eis asked Gorski.

"Scans are indicating all clear," Gorski said as he finished the last of fifteen large tanks. "Fire them up."

Jan Eis smiled and began typing on the large desktop computer before her. "Everything is still operational. Doctor Jin-Woo should be igniting the engines as we speak."

Gorski and Harrison looked around as they heard a loud set of booms from direction of the engine room. The Battle Cruiser *Cleopatra* shook violently as the massive hybrid engine came to life. Gorski realized he was smiling at Jan Eis.

She was smiling back at him in a flirtatious manner, "So, Lieutenant Narc, don't you have to go secure the Command Station on level one?"

Gorski laughed at himself for being taken in so

easily by the beauty of Jan Eis. He walked out into the hallway and motioned for eleven marines to follow him. Gorski led the squad up the fifteen foot wide and height east hall away from the engine room toward the large staircase. The doors to the staircase were sliding doors, about twenty feet wide. He ordered the computer to slide open the entrance of the staircase. As the doors slid open, Gorski aimed his laser rifle upwards and noticed that the first flight of stairs was empty. He led the Marines inside and slowly ascended the stairs, taking one step at a time. Gorski remembered to breathe as he had to pace himself on the walk upward for forty flights of stairs. The ceiling in the stairwell was fifteen feet high and the stairs were twenty feet wide, to allow for extra space for emergencies. The stairs themselves were the color of the United Nations Flag, alternating orange, baby blue, white and black. On the left side of the stairs were grey metal walls, with an occasional computer panel connected to the wall to request assistance, declare an emergency or communicate with other parts of the massive Battle Cruiser. When Gorski made it to the third level, he realized that Doctor Erik Macinlock was walking next to him.

"This is my stop," Macinlock told Gorski. "Do you mind lending me two marines to clear the medical area?"

"Not at all, sir. I will give you five," Gorski motioned to closest five women, one sergeant and four private's. "Escort the good doctor to the medical area. Stay with him until further notice."

"Yes sir," the sergeant said as she opened the door to the third level. They led the doctor out of the stairwell and into the hallway.

Gorski continued to lead the other six marines up the staircase. When they reached the second level and the location of the main weapons section, they found a decapitated body lying on the metal stairs. Blood was everywhere but there was no sign of the severed head. Gorski inspected the headless corpse. The deceased was a male, with the rank insignia of Commander, in a dark blue uniform. He had been the chief pilot of the *Cleopatra*.

"Gorski to Lieutenant Shigeta," Gorski noticed that the corpse had a large wound in his chest, about where the heart would be located. "We found the chief pilot of the Cleopatra. His head is missing and he has a massive chest wound. Dried blood is everywhere."

There was a pause before Shigeta responded. "We have found several other high ranking officers as well, in the same condition. So far we have a total of eight decapitated bodies. Keep heading for Level One, and

Gorksi?"

"Sir?"

"Can you fly this ship?"

Gorski was the one to pause now; he hoped he would not regret his willingness to volunteer. He had trained to fly a Battle Cruiser at the Academy. But he had never actually done so, other than in computer simulators. "Sir, yes sir."

"Good," Shigeta responded. "The engines are working, life support is functional. I am sending Harrison up to Weapons to secure that area. When you arrive at the Command Station, I need you to get the Cleopatra parallel to the Cortez. We are going on a long trip."

"Where to, sir?" Gorski kept walking.

"Top secret," Shigeta said quickly. "I will be up there soon with Lieutenant Vela and verbally inform you of the coordinates. Shigeta out."

Gorski kept walking up the stair case. He did not blame Shigeta for being so vague. The other ship had hostile crew members. If the *Cleopatra* had similar undetected crew, then they could very well be monitoring their communications. Gorski kept walking, aiming his laser rifle upwards. He finally made it to the top of the stairs. He was breathing heavily as were the other soldiers with him.

Gorski looked at Lance Corporal Pool who standing next to him. "I am going to order the computer to open the sliding doors. Once I do that, I need you to enter the Command Station with me. You sweep to the right and I'll go left."

"Yes sir," Pool affirmed that she understood. She held a laser rifle in her arms, ready for action.

Gorski looked to the other Marines, "I want you to follow us in, one at a time, count to ten before entering. If we are in a laser fight, take cover and back us up, if we are still alive."

"Yes sir!" The remaining marines said in unison.

Gorski loved the Marines. He admired their approach to the military, their discipline and comradery. As a so-called military brat, Gorski had been afforded many opportunities to observe the Marines.

Gorski stared at the entrance. On the facade above the grey, metallic sliding doors were the words in red bold letters "COMMAND STATION."

Gorski looked over the Marines one last time. His breathing had calmed from the long walk upstairs. Gorski tightened his grip on his laser rifle. "Computer, open the east stairwell entrance to the Command Station."

The doors slid open, giving them an eight foot wide and ten foot high entrance. The lights were not working, so Gorski ordered his enviro-suit to activate his lights on his helmet and Pool did the same. The lighting from the Gorski walked in to the left, aiming his weapon. Pool swept the room on the right. They swept the upper walk way and found two decapitated bodies of Space Command officers on the floor, dried blood spattered everywhere. Gorski walked to the first row of seats which were designated for the Admiral, the Captain and the Executive Officer.

Gorski rounded the corner and was facing the three seats. Two were empty. The Captain's chair had a headless body seated in it, with a short sword embedded in the chest of the corpse. Gorski could see that the rest of his team had entered the room and were moving swiftly to occupy the upper walkways. Gorski inspected the corpse in the Captain's seat. He read the name tag on the black Class A uniform. It read "Al-Bashir."

"Sir, there are three other bodies over here," a marine reported standing near the pilot's command chair and the Astral Navigation chair. "All officers."

Gorski knew he had found Captain Faisal al-Bashir, one of the highest decorated Captain's in the Space Command.

"Gorski to Shigeta."

"Shigeta here. Report."

"Sir, we have the Command Station. We found Captain al-Bashir. He's dead as are many of his top officers. No sign of Admiral Cardenas." Gorski informed Shigeta. Gorski smiled as the lights came on in the Command Station and the power began to make a humming noise. The *Cleopatra* was now fully operational.

"Good work, Gorski." Shigeta said. "Professor Brennan reports that the ship is biologically safe. Everyone can now remove their enviro-suits. Mister Gorski, take the pilot's seat. Get us next to the Cortez and I will be up soon."

"Yes sir," Gorski set down his laser rifle and removed his enviro-suit helmet. He inspected the pilot's seat. He was relieved that there was not any blood there. He and the Marines in his team began shedding their enviro-suits.

Gorski looked over the other dead bodies. High ranking officers stabbed in the chest and decapitated. He saw many other bodies with their bones obliterated. Their fleshy remains in piles that reminded Gorski of piles of crap from farm animals, except these were all flesh toned. He wondered what the hell happened. He sat down and began powering up the pilot command computer desk. As he did so he and his Marines were stunned to hear a voice.

"Hello my friends!"

Gorski looked up and reached for his laser rifle on the floor at his feet. He saw a light red life size image of Admiral Cardenas before him. The image looked as if the Admiral were actually standing before them, but it was merely a projection, a pre-recorded message left for someone to find. Gorski had seen pictures of the Admiral before at the house of his dead friend, Porfirio Cardenas. Admiral Cardenas had been Porfirio's father.

The image continued to speak: "I am Admiral Cardenas. If you have boarded this ship, the Cleopatra, you have found that she was abandoned. I, and those loyal to me, have left the Cleopatra and Tonkin Gulf behind so that our story could be discovered. Many of you may know that my son, Porfirio, had been a cadet at Clovis Academy. He died on the moon orbiting planet Semiramis during the so-called Blood Moon Incident. My son died because our Glorious Leader, Vladimir Sikorsky, arranged for the ambush and murder of Porfirio and his friends. I have proof that the Glorious Leader was involved, which is why I have joined the rebellion against him. After you hear the remainder of this recording, I hope that each of you will join us to create a more perfect union for the people of Earth."

By now, the elevator lift to the Command Station had opened and Shigeta, Brennan, Vela and another Marine entered. They had heard the last two sentences of Admiral Cardenas. Vela silently sat down in the astral navigation seat, next to Gorski, her eyes wide with amazement. Shigeta sat in the Admiral's seat. They all listened as Cardenas told them his evidence against the Royal Family.

CHAPTER SEVEN

The bodies of Captain Faisal al-Bashir, Captain Natalia Sikorsky, Captain Arvidas Sikorsky, Captain Thomas Tsukifuji and Captain Trini Urbanczyk were all confirmed by Doctor Erik Macinlock and his nurses after the DNA test results were received from the main computer. All of the Captains had been decapitated and their hearts had been run through by short sword. After the two Battle Cruisers had been thoroughly searched, there were over eighty dead bodies found on the Tonkin Gulf and the Cleopatra, the vast majority of which were headless bodies of officers related to the Glorious Leader. The other bodies found on the two Battle Cruisers were those of men and women of various ranks, with their bone structure completely obliterated by the new weapons recovered by Lieutenant Dominic Andolini.

After the security sweeps of both of the abandoned space ships, Admiral Weems ordered more pilots and engineers to be sent to assist in making the *Tonkin Gulf* and *Cleopatra* ready for battle. Additional computer technicians and other technical crew were sent as well, to give Captain Sowa more personnel options.

The MI soldiers that Dominic had faced down were transferred to the *Cleopatra* so that Macinlock and his nurses could surgically remove the mind control micro-chips from their brains. The theory was that the soldiers, after they recovered from the procedure, would be able to enlighten them as to what had happened to the rest of the Fleet.

Captain Sowa ordered that Dominic, with the assistance of Gorski, Harrison, Shigeta, Jason Allen and Jan Eis, dissect one of the new weapons and find out as much as possible regarding its operation, power source, origin and the form of caliber or elements used to inflict the damage that had been observed. The officers did as instructed and in their investigation of the weapon they discovered a power pack of some form of plasma that none of them had ever seen before.

"It is alien in design and the source of the weapon is also foreign," Jan Eis remarked as she carefully inspected the rectangular plastic cartridge that had the matter inside.

"A burst from that and your bones get dissolved?" Harrison shook his head. "Whoever created this was one sick bastard."

Dominic nodded in agreement with that comment. He watched his two men die and heard their screams as the deadly plasma crushed their bones into nothing. "Believe me, you do not want to be hit by that weapon."

"How many did we recover in the two Battle Cruisers?" Shigeta asked turning to Gorski.

"We found forty of these weapons," Gorski told them. "I had our Marines secure them in the weapons storage room on the Cleopatra. I ordered two armed guards to watch over them, just in case we missed some other combatants during our sweeps of the ships."

"Impossible," Harrison barked. "We went to every room, every section, and every hallway. There is no one left to fight us."

"Even if we did get everyone, Gorski is correct in taking precautions," Shigeta told them. "Lieutenant

Harcourt, have you been able to repair the engine room to handle full, battle condition operations?"

"We are partially ready," Jan Eis responded. "I could use some more help in the Engine and life support sections. Perhaps you could request that Admiral Weems assign us some more crew members. When they abandoned these two ships, they intentionally damaged some of the ability of the Tonkin Gulf and Cleopatra to reach maximum speed and maneuvering capability. We are still addressing those issues. I could use a security presence as well. Most of my staff are scientists, not soldiers. If Gorski is correct that there may be a few combatants still on board, the most likely location to stage an attack would be the engine room."

"Right, they could control the entire ship from the engine section." Gorski nodded. "And they could kill all of us by cutting off the oxygen supplies to the rest of the craft. I could take a few Marines and set them up to protect the engineering staff. Just in case."

"Do it," Shigeta ordered. "Andolini, I want you and Allen to go back to the Tonkin Gulf and stay glued to the side of Captain Sowa. Protect her at all costs."

"Yes sir," Dominic responded.

"Harrison, stay with Doctor Macinlock and protect

him. He claims he found something interesting in some of the men and women we found on the ship." Shigeta was speaking softly so that no one else could hear their conversation. "Some of them had micro-chips in their brains. Macinlock thinks they were some form of mind control. If he is on to something, then he might be ambushed to shut him up."

"Are the computer chips similar to the ones we found on the Saharakaree that attacked us on the Blood Moon?" Harrison raised his eyebrows as he asked the question.

"That is what we need to find out," Shigeta told them. "Let's move out, people."

Dominic and Allen departed together to make their way back to the Raumschiff and fly back to the Tonkin Gulf.

Gorski followed the lovely Jan Eis out into the hallway and toward the large stairwell at the end. They walked into the stairwell, after the sliding doors opened for them. Jan stopped abruptly, turned and embraced Gorski. Her lips found his and she pushed him against the wall as Gorski kissed her back with passion. He wrapped his arms around her, holding her tight.

"You aren't concerned with anyone walking in and

catching us?" Gorski asked, in between kisses.

Jan Eis smiled at him and ran her fingers through his hair. "Not in the slightest. There are only a hundred of us on the entire ship. We are virtually alone."

They continued kissing and running their hands over each other's bodies. She took Gorski by the hand and led him down the stairs about five steps down. She stopped and began unzipping her engineering uniform. Gorski also removed his clothing and they pulled each other down onto the stairs and they made love.

After both had climaxed from their passion. They remained on the metal stairs for a few moments, holding each other and kissing softly.

"Have you ever been with one of us?" Jan-Eis asked. "I mean a child of Athena?"

"You are the first," Gorski told her.

"So, what did you think? Was I better than the normal human female?"

Gorski nodded, "You are amazing. You, um, didn't use your powers to seduce me or anything? I mean, this was all my own desires for you, right?"

She squinted her eyes and looked into his. "You have had friends controlled by a Harcourt in the past? Is it okay if I read your mind?"

Gorski shrugged, "Go ahead."

Jan Eis reached up with both her hands and touched Gorski's face. He watched her as she smiled and began speaking in a low monotone voice. "Your friend, Drayton Love-Easter was used by one of my distant relatives. She seduced him, using her pheromones. She caused him to lose his woman, Yesenia. His child. A son. I see their faces through your memories. They were all emotionally damaged from the violation by the female Harcourt."

She stopped speaking and cuddled into Gorski's arms. "I promise to never do that to you, Yuri Gorski. We may look similar, but we Harcourt's are all different. I won't do anything to bring you harm."

"I know." Gorski held her close to him, enjoying the warmth of her body next to his. "You do seem special, wonderful and you are so beautiful. I don't want to be apart from you."

"And Laura Murdock? She is far lovelier than I could ever be. What happens when you see her again? You would choose me over her?"

Gorski nodded, "I just did choose you over her by making love to you. Murdock was fun, but I sense she is trouble. I know I can trust you completely. With her, I never felt comfortable."

"But you were okay with having sex with her."

Gorski smiled, "That was before I had gotten to know you better."

"Good. Because I am yours, Yuri Gorski. My body is yours. My heart and soul belong to you. I knew it from the moment I met you that you were my love of my life."

"Because you saw me coming in one of your dreams about the future?"

Jan Eis smiled and kissed him. "Yes, I did. I dreamed about this, about you, several years ago. All the way back to when I was a child. I saw your face. In my dreams I would feel you make love to me. When I saw you on the news reports about the Blood Moon I felt my heart skip. I knew I had found my destiny."

"That is a big responsibility to live up to ones dreams. How did I...perform?"

She laughed and kissed Gorski again. "Having you in person was so much better than my dreams. I want you to make love to me every day and night."

"I am sure I can rise to the challenge," Gorski said as he stood up and then lifted her into his arms. "We had better get to the engine section before people start asking questions."

"Jerry Goodman is there. I am certain everything is

under control." She found her one-piece uniform and began dressing. She could not stop smiling.

For some reason, Gorski found that he was also smiling. He felt happy. Perhaps Jan Eis was his destiny. Making love with her felt right, as if it were meant to be.

The two lovers held hands as they slowly descended the long stair case, laughing and kissing as they walked.

In the engine room Jerry Goodman watched the two female computer technicians and three female engineers continue their duties, conducting systems checks and running diagnostics on the hybrid solar and nuclear engine. There were two female Marine Corps Privates at the entrance to the engine room. Each held a laser rifle in their arms and were pacing back and forth. Goodman liked the fact that women out numbered men. It made the odds for sex that much better for him. He began looking over his choices of the seven women in his immediate location. All were in decent physical condition. All seemed attractive in their own way. He decided on the female Asian engineer in the far corner of the massive room. She had joined the crew of the *Cortez* just a year earlier. Goodman thought her name was Brenda Wong and that she had been a child prodigy, one of those brilliant kids that learn at an accelerated rate. Wong was just nineteen years old and had a Doctorate in Nuclear Engineering, a Master's Degree in Advanced Space Craft Design and a Bachelor's Degree in Mechanical Engineering. Goodman decided he would give her the pleasure of breeding with a member of the Royal Family by the end of the work shift. A smart, educated girl like Brenda Wong would not refuse such a gracious offer.

Goodman felt his hand held communication device buzzing. He reached down with his right hand and removed it from his belt loop. He noticed the face on the screen was that of Anastasia Sikorsky. She had joined Goodman on board the U.N.S.C. *Cleopatra* to assist in the weapons room in case of an attack.

"Yes?" Goodman answered with a whisper as to not disturb the others.

"Jerry, trouble." Anastasia whispered as well. "Word is that rebellions against our family are occurring all over the eight solar systems. We are being hunted down to extinction. They killed all of our family members on the Martian Colonies. Several Territories on old Earth are doing the same. It is serious."

"What should we do, then?" Goodman was a bit worried now. He had heard the reports of Royal Family members being found decapitated. He was in no mood to have his head chopped off. As a member of the Royal

Family it was his right to live forever, a right he intended to enjoy to the fullest.

"I spoke to Doctor Sowa and Murdock. We are to take control of the ships," Anastasia instructed softly, walking around the Weapons Section of the *Cleopatra*. Lying at her feet were fifteen dead technicians and three Weapons Officers whose limbs had been ripped from their bodies. Anastasia ambushed them and easily murdered them before contacting Goodman. "Kill everyone."

"Right now?" Goodman raised his voice a little and looked around the room nervously to see if anyone had overheard the conversation.

"Right now," Anastasia ordered. "I will see you on the Command Station after we wipe out everyone on the lower levels."

Goodman watched as Anastasia's face faded from his view screen. He shrugged and set down his small communication device and sighed. He walked over to another row of computers on the bottom row of the engine room. Underneath the desks was a hand laser he had securely taped for future use. He reached under the computer console and fished around with his right hand until he found the weapon. He pulled it loose of the tape and checked the settings level. He set it on kill and turned toward the two female Marines at the entrance.

They were both pretty young girls. Too bad they had to be eliminated. But, orders were orders. Goodman fired at the nearest Marine and his laser blast opened a hole in her back that exploded out the front of her chest. Before the second Marine could react Goodman fired at her, causing the young woman's head to explode, spattering brains and skull chunks all over the walls and floors.

The computer technicians and the engineers behind Goodman began screaming and trying to find a place to hide. Goodman began firing at the defenseless women. One of the computer technicians lost her left leg first before she was hit in the abdomen by another deadly blast. One of the female engineers was climbing up the ladders to get up high, and hopefully out of range of Goodman's laser fire. She calculated wrong as Goodman fired up at her, severing her right arm from her body. She screamed as she plummeted to the metal floor below.

Goodman killed them all except for the Asian engineer named Brenda Wong. He aimed his laser at her as she cowered against a row of computer banks. She was shaking with fear, tears flowing down her cheeks.

"Please. Don't kill me," she pleaded with him.

Goodman smiled at her. She was very pretty and

Anastasia did not say anything about restrictions in how long it took to kill everyone. He was going to have a little fun with Wong. "Take off your clothes. If you pleasure me, I might allow you to live."

Goodman watched as the woman slowly complied, peeling off her civilian clothing as Goodman began to hum some song that she had never heard before. He cared little that Wong was sobbing as she undressed. As a member of the Royal Family, Goodman had been raised to see all non-Royal humans as mere livestock. The women were there to reproduce for him and his siblings. They were the herds that were to perpetuate the human race and then sacrifice their body parts for aging Royal Family members.

Goodman enjoyed the view as Wong removed her clothing. She was almost completely naked when Goodman heard something behind him at the Engine Room entrance.

"Drop your weapon or you are dead," Yuri Gorski told him. He had his weapon ready, due to the gruesome sight of the two Marine Corps soldiers dead at the entrance. Gorski deduced that the guards had been ambushed.

Goodman turned his head and saw that Gorski was aiming a laser rifle at him. The MI Lieutenant was standing behind the headless body of one of the female Marines. Behind Gorski was the Child of Athena, Jan Eis Harcourt.

Gorski did not understand why Goodman would go crazy and kill the other crew members. Perhaps there was something about the ship that caused crew members to lose it. Or Goodman had some mental health issues that had gone undetected by the required annual psychiatric evaluations. Gorski and Jan Eis arrived to see the blasted bodies of the women on the floor. Since Goodman was holding the last survivor at gun point, it was safe to assume he was the one that killed everyone.

"I said, drop it!" Gorski ordered loudly.

"You drop your weapon or I kill the girl." Goodman kept his weapon on the half-naked Asian engineer. "I really don't want to have to kill her, she is so very hot. But if you force me to, I will do it."

"Yuri, he is a Sikorsky." Jan Eis whispered. She was reading Goodman's mind, using her special Child of Athena powers. "He was told to kill us all."

"By who?" Gorski whispered.

"By me," a voice echoed in the hallway.

It was Anastasia Sikorsky. She had just finished murdering all of the crew men and women that had been sent to serve in the weapons section. Anastasia had planned on going to the medical area next but then thought better of that due to her knowledge that Goodman was a sexual predator. She was glad she followed her instincts to go to the engine room first. The idiot Goodman let his deviant sexual desires get in the way of killing everyone as she had instructed.

Anastasia had on her one piece uniform with vision intensifier goggles and special hearing aids that enabled her to hear sounds from great distances. Underneath her uniform was a new piece of technology, called a reflector vest. It was similar to a bullet proof vest, but its' purpose was to repel any laser blast that might hit her in the chest or mid-section. She had straps over her shoulders connected to a web belt. The belt had two laser pistols attached to it as well as a knife and several grenades.

Anastasia fired her laser rifle at Gorski and Jan Eis. Gorski grabbed Jan Eis by her arm and pulled her into the engine room and behind the protective metal walls to avoid being hit. The laser blasts impacted the entrance facade and sizzled with energy and sparks on impact. Gorski pushed Jan Eis behind a row of computer desks for her protection and took aim at Goodman. Goodman kicked Wong aside and threw himself to the ground and tried to aim at Gorski and Jan Eis.

But Goodman was too late. Gorski fired his laser rifle and Goodman screamed as his body was blown in half.

His legs were tossed into the air several feet and then crumpled to the floor. What was left of his chest and head followed and slammed to the metal floor, just inches from where Wong was cowering.

Gorski did not hesitate. He rolled over and over to get behind one of the remains of a female computer technician. He watched as Anastasia dived behind the thick facade, where he could not get off a clean shot at her.

"Gorski!" Anastasia yelled over the rumble of the hybrid engine. She had recognized him from his famous performance on the Blood Moon. Gorski and Harrison were the only two crew members of the *Cleopatra* that had concerned her. They were both brave men that would fight like wild cats until they were dead. They both proved that they did not know the meaning of the word defeat. "If you two surrender I will let you live! The Royal Family has no quarrel with you! Throw down your laser rifle! We can discuss your future as a Captain of your own ship!"

"How can I trust you?" Gorski yelled back, hoping that by engaging her in conversation she would be distracted long enough for help to arrive.

"I am a Royal Family member!" Anastasia answered him. "I can grant you any wish that you want! Your own Captaincy! Women, all you can handle and more! Empire Dollars in amounts that most humans never see in a lifetime. I can even give you immortality!"

Gorski looked over to Jan Eis. He felt her thoughts enter his head. "Yuri, she is lying. She will kill us if we surrender."

Gorski tried to send his thoughts back to Jan Eis. "Is she desperate enough to blast the nuclear engine and kill everyone on the ship?"

Jan Eis was able to read his thoughts. She responded in the negative to that question. Gorski heard her voice in his head explain that Anastasia would not take any chances with her own life.

Gorski watched the engine room entrance like a hawk, expecting Anastasia to charge in firing at any moment. Gorski was surprised when the half-naked Asian engineer slid next to him. She was holding the laser pistol that Jerry Goodman had used to murder the other women in the engine room. Her eyes were still wide with fear.

"Thank you," she told him softly.

"You are welcome," Gorski whispered back as he kept his eyes focused on the entrance.

Gorski cursed when he observed two thermite grenades rolling into the engine room.

"Take cover!" Gorski screamed at Jan Eis and

Wong.

The two women dived behind computer panels as Gorski threw the carcass of one of the computer technicians on top of one of the grenades. He dived toward the nuclear engine as the two explosives detonated. Balls of fire expanded outward from the explosions. The remains of the female technician that Gorski tossed on top of one of the explosives were vaporized in the eruption of white hot flames. The temperature in the engine room went up about ten degrees which would certainly alert the officers on the Command Station on the First Level of the *Cleopatra*.

Gorski kept his bearings directed at the engine room entrance, expecting Anastasia to charge in, firing her weapon. But after several tense seconds, Gorski realized there would be no attack.

"She's gone," Jan Eis said as she crawled out from behind the computer panel she had been hiding behind. "I kept my mind locked with hers. She was planning on killing everyone in the medical station next."

Gorski ran to the entrance, pointing his laser rifle down the long hallway to the north. He looked to the right and left, satisfying himself that the Sikorsky woman was gone. He turned back to Jan Eis and the other woman.

"What is your name?" Gorski asked as he picked up

one of the laser rifles that had been in the possession of the female Marines killed by Jerry Goodman.

"Wong. Brenda Wong," The engineer answered.

"Okay, you two stay here and protect the engine room." Gorski tossed the laser rifle to Jan Eis. "Contact Drew and Doctor Macinlock. Warn them that the Sikorsky woman is on her way and should be killed on sight. Then warn the Command Station."

"What are you going to do?" Jan Eis demanded as she caught the laser rifle.

"I am going to track her down," Gorski smiled at her. "Seal the protective bulkheads behind me."

Jan Eis watched as Gorski began sprinting down the north hallway from the engine room entrance.

"What a hunk," Wong said, watching Gorski run down the hall. "Where do we get a man like that?"

Jan Eis laughed and ran to the communication system to follow Gorski's instructions. Anastasia Sikorsky was a cold blooded killer, just as Goldman had been. Drew Harrison must be alerted to the pending attack.

"I will contact the medical and command areas," Jan Eis told Wong. "Seal the bulkheads as Gorski ordered."

"But you outrank him," Wong observed.

"True, but his orders are correct. We have to secure the engine room." Jan Eis advised Wong. She watched as Gorski moved down the metal hallway and hoped he would make it back to her safe.

Gorski walked rapidly, remembering his training at Spetsnaz, not to rush to his own death. He kept the laser rifle pointing in the direction of his movement, his eyes darting back and forth waiting for Anastasia to charge out at him at any moment. He heard the bulkheads to the engine room slam shut behind him. Gorski was certain the woman would have gone up the stairs at the end of the north hallway. That would be the quickest way to get to the medical section and where Macinlock and his nurses were working.

Gorski ran to the stairwell entrance and found a dead female Marine on the floor. Her throat had been slit open; her blood was spread all over the walls and the metal floor. The poor girl must have been on duty, patrolling the ship when Sikorsky ran into her.

Gorski cautiously peered around the stairwell entrance, pointing the laser rifle up stairs and then down, looking for any signs of movement or trip wires. Seeing none, he walked into the stairwell and slowly began to ascend, keeping his back against the wall and his gaze upwards at all times. He moved silently. If Sikorsky was waiting for him, Gorski did not want to give her any clues as to his whereabouts.

Harrison had been standing guard at the medical station, pacing back and forth. His thoughts muddled with his recent personal errors in judgment. He had not been able to muster the courage to confess to Gorski that he had sex with Murdock and he had not been able to get LaShondra Lewis to speak to him at all. Harrison was certain he had caused irreparable damage to his relationship with Lewis. He feared the same might be true of his friendship to Gorski.

Harrison watched as Doctor Macinlock and several of his nurses worked on removing a computer microchip from the brain of one of the MI soldiers that Dominic had encountered. It seemed that the attackers were all being controlled remotely by some unknown person. Harrison wondered what kind of diabolical mind would devise such a method of mind control. Harrison could think of nothing worse than losing self-control.

He smiled at the female Marine that was on guard duty with him. She was a decent looking young lady, sporting the rank of Lance Corporal on the arms of her camouflaged, one piece, Class C uniform. Her name tag read Foray. She had a laser rifle in her arms and was pacing back and forth, just as Harrison had been. Harrison wondered what Lewis was doing at that moment. He knew she was on the *Tonkin Gulf*, probably performing the same type of duty.

Harrison was about to say something to Foray when he saw the woman thrown across the room, her chest exploding. Foray did not even have a chance to scream. Whoever had shot her did so from the back. The female Marine was dead before she hit the ground.

"Doctor! Get down!" Harrison yelled to Macinlock. Harrison slid to his knees and aimed at the entrance to the medical station, scanning the large room left to right, up and down.

He saw nothing.

Harrison crawled on his hands and knees, keeping his laser rifle aimed down the hallway. He hoped that Macinlock and his nurses were behind something secure. He could hear the warnings over the computer-communications system of the *Cleopatra* from Jan Eis that Anastasia was on a murderous rampage. Harrison cursed to himself. First the large amount of family members from the Rosenburg's wanted them all dead. Then the Ragnarsson's and now the Sikorsky's. Harrison moved slowly to the right and thought he observed movement out of the corner of his eye on the left.

He swung the barrel of his laser rifle in the direction of the movement. But he was too late. Anastasia fired her laser rifle in his direction. Her shot was rushed so she missed Harrison, but her blast did hit his laser rifle causing the weapon to be rendered into several useless pieces. Both of his hands suffered burns from the laser blast.

Harrison snarled at his being seen and almost being killed. He rolled to his right as Anastasia attempted to fire on him again. Harrison slid behind a large metal hospital bed that was on roller wheels. He kicked the bed in her direction.

"Shit!" Anastasia screamed as the bed rolled at her. She did her best to jump out of the way, but the bed clipped her on the side. She slid to the ground, tumbling over and over toward the direction of the medical staff.

She saw Macinlock directing his nurses to get to one of the emergency exits. Anastasia smiled and aimed at Macinlock with her laser rifle. She fired.

Doctor Erik Macinlock, brilliant surgeon and a friend of many, died as his upper torso exploded into pieces of flesh, bone and meat. The three nurses screamed as small separated body parts of Macinlock hit them in the face and other parts of their body. Anastasia was certain her cousin, Laura, would be upset that one of her toy boys was dead.

Harrison had been running at full speed at Anastasia at the same time she pulled the trigger for her kill shot on Macinlock. She attempted to turn her laser rifle in his direction but was not fast enough. Harrison's body crashed into hers, the force of the impact causing both of them to slam into the wall. She fell to the ground with Harrison on top of her. Harrison hit her twice in the face with his left hand and quickly realized he was in trouble.

Anastasia laughed maniacally as Harrison cried out in pain. He held his left hand, which was now broken from hitting her face, which was reinforced by a solid metal skull and jaw. What Harrison did not know was that Anastasia had replaced her entire bone structure with metallic alloys. Her skin was from many young girls that were skinned alive to provide her with natural feeling skin. With little effort, she flipped Harrison into the air with her metallic arms.

Harrison screamed out a curse word as he flew over ten feet into the air and crashed onto the top of several operating tables. One of the tables flipped over due to the impact with Harrison's body weight. Harrison slammed to the floor on his back. He could hear Anastasia laughing at his misery, taunting him while he was down.

Harrison pushed himself to his feet and screamed out loud from the sharp pain he felt when he placed weight on his broken left hand. He looked up toward the laughing Anastasia. He shook his head to make certain he was not hallucinating. His adversary was growing in size before his very eyes, just as David Rosenburg had done on the Blood Moon. She glared at Harrison as her metal legs grew, stretching her to about seven and a half feet tall. Anastasia lifted her arms to the ceiling and continued her mad laugh as the sides of her torso opened up.

"Ah, shit!" Harrison said as he watched four metallic arms slowly spread out from Anastasia's rib cage area. She now had three arms on her right and the same number on her left. Each of the newly revealed arms were solid metal and longer than her normal arms, giving her additional reach in combat.

Harrison spied upon his laser pistol lying on the hospital floor. He rolled toward his weapon. He was surprised that Anastasia did not pounce on him.

But as he took hold of the laser in his right hand and turned to face the woman with the metallic bone structure he saw the reason why she had not finished him off.

Anastasia had been using her multiple mechanical arms to crush the skulls of the MI patients that Macinlock had been operating on. One by one she leapt next to the beds where the sleeping men were and used her fists as battering rams to smash their heads into oblivion. Harrison grimaced at the sight of crushed skulls and oozing brain matter dripping onto the floor. Harrison fired his weapon at her and cursed as his laser beams bounced off of her, reflecting back in Harrison's direction. He rolled to his right to avoid being hit by the very energy beams that he had fired.

Once the unconscious patients of the medical area had been killed, Anastasia turned her attention to the closest nurse to her. Harrison watched in disbelief as Anastasia picked up the nurse with her six arms. The other two nurses were screaming in terror as they watched the six arms of Anastasia tear the struggling nurse to pieces. First her arms and legs were ripped from her body. At some point, the victim ceased her death cries. Anastasia then finished the unfortunate nurse by grabbing her rib cage and splitting it open. The flesh tore and blood was spattered all over the medical area. Harrison could hear the sickening crushing of the bones of the victims.

Harrison fired his hand laser three times at the Sikorsky woman. His laser blasts burned through clothing and flesh, but did nothing to the metallic bone structure. Most of the shots ricocheted off her body and hit the walls, leaving burn marks behind.

Anastasia tossed the carcass of the dead nurse in her six hands to the floor and turned her attention to Harrison. "Your weapons mean nothing! I am invincible and immortal! I am a Goddess! You will all die." She began moving toward one of the other screaming nurses.

Harrison growled and picked up a heavy metallic four foot wide and three foot tall machine that was used to sterilize hospital instruments for surgery. He threw the apparatus with all of his strength in the direction of Sikorsky. The metallic sterilizer clanged onto Anastasia's head, causing her to lose her balance and fall against the eastern wall of the medical section.

As Anastasia struggled to her feet, Harrison waved to the two surviving nurses to run. One of the young nurses did not need to be told; she crawled to her feet and ran as fast as she ever had in her life out the door and out into the hallway. The second nurse was too paralyzed with fear to move. She sat in a fetal position sobbing like a baby.

Harrison pushed his momentary advantage and lifted up a metal operating bed and charged at Anastasia. As she was regaining her balance, Harrison slammed the table into her left side, sending her stumbling to the floor. Harrison dropped the bed and ran to the petrified nurse and grabbed her right arm with his right hand. He threw the woman over his shoulder and turned to run.

Harrison saw out of the corner of his eyes that Anastasia was now on all eight of her mechanical limbs and was charging toward him like a spider. Harrison had no choice but to drop the nurse to the floor and begin firing his laser pistol at her. Each shot fired did not slow her pace.

"Fool!" Anastasia taunted him as she scurried across the floor at him. "You killed my uncle Alfred! My cousins David, Caine and Daryl! Did you think that we would never seek out our revenge? After I finish you I will find your friends and tear them to shreds. Gorski will suffer the worst when I get my hands on him!"

Harrison braced himself for the inevitable impact. His laser was useless. He was not anywhere near any other metal objects to use to throw at her. He swallowed hard ready to embrace death. He hoped that he could delay the Sikorsky woman enough so that the nurses would have time to escape.

But Anastasia did not reach him. To his delight, Harrison watched as Anastasia Sikorsky was hit by a blast from a laser rifle in her left side. She was sent sliding several feet until she collided with the metal wall. The sound of the collision was loud. The impact left the metal wall bent in several places.

Harrison turned to the entrance to see Yuri Gorski standing there with his laser rifle aimed at Anastasia. Gorski kept firing into the woman as she screamed under the barrage of deadly laser fire. Her flesh was being blown off of her metallic skin with each blast.

"Drew, get her out of here!" Gorski motioned with his head at the nurse on the floor.

Harrison scooped the nurse up with his right arm and ran past Gorski.

"Man I could kiss you right now!" Harrison yelled as he ran toward the entrance.

The now flesh-less Anastasia Sikorsky stood up on her elongated metallic legs and began to advance on Gorski. He continued to fire upon her, each shot from his laser rifle caused her to fall back a half step. But with each half step she fell back she advanced two steps toward him.

Gorski was uncertain of what form of metal alloys she had used to construct her skeletal design, but it was strong enough to deflect the energy of a laser pistol and laser rifle. To win against the Sikorsky woman, traditional weaponry would not work. Gorski backed out of the medical station, slowly, firing at the Sikorsky woman over and over again. When he made it to the facade of the entrance to the medical station, Gorski ordered the computer for the *Cleopatra* to seal the secondary metal bulkheads. The five foot thick metal doors came crashing down from the ceiling of the medical station to the floor, separating Gorski from Anastasia Sikorsky. He could hear her roar with rage.

"That was great!" Harrison told Gorski. "Now what?"

They could hear the banging on the bulkheads by Anastasia. She was attempting to break through.

"Metal conducts heat," Gorski told his friend. "Her internal organs and her brain are under that metal skeletal shell. We raise the temperature on her and she burns alive, internally."

"Ah, that is really wicked." Harrison said, holding his left hand gingerly in his right.

"Computer, sterilize the medical station with intensified heat. Raise the temperature in that station to five hundred degrees Fahrenheit." Gorski instructed.

"Temperature is rising," the computer responded.

In the medical station Anastasia Sikorsky felt the intense heat flooding in through the vents. She screamed, realizing what was happening. She tried to communicate with Gorski and Harrison, to offer surrender. But the two men refused to respond to her pleas.

Anastasia Sikorsky let out several screams as her blood began to boil inside her metal skeletal structure. Her brain cooked in the rising heat. Her metallic outer skeleton crashed to the floor as she died.

James Shigeta soon arrived on the scene with Brennan and Vela. Shigeta and Vela had their laser pistols drawn and were ready for action. Brennan assisted the two surviving nurses in looking over Harrison's injured hand. After Gorski gave Shigeta and Vela a quick statement of the events that occurred in the medical and engine sections Shigeta decided on some new precautions.

"Vela get back to the Command Station," Shigeta told the pilot. "Until further notice, you are in command. We can no longer trust our communication systems if we have traitors on board. We have to communicate face to face or use your personal communication devices."

"Yes sir," Vela nodded and began to leave.

"Wait, I am not finished." Shigeta told Vela. "After Professor Brennan and the remaining staff here fix up Harrison's hand, he is to be your body guard. You go nowhere unless he is glued to your side. Understand?"

"Yes I understand," Vela was a bit angry that Shigeta would assume she could not defend herself. But the idea of a human transforming into an indestructible metal spider was, to say the least, a cause for concern.

"Gorski, contact Andolini on your personal holo-com. Warn him about what occurred. His pilot, Jason Allen can be trusted. But there is a co-pilot, a Lieutenant French, and I do not know him. So make sure he understands that what you have to tell him is absolutely confidential." Shigeta slapped Gorski on the back.

"Got it, sir." Gorski began to pull out his holo-com from his pouch that was attached to his utility belt to warn his friend Dominic of the dangers that might be waiting for him at the *Tonkin Gulf.*

"And get back to the Engine Room," Shigeta ordered Gorski. "Harcourt and Wong are our only two engineering experts on the ship. Jin-Woo already went back to the Cortez. So, we need those two women alive."

"Yes sir," Gorski responded.

"And Gorski, you are going to be up for an accommodation for your actions today." Shigeta said to the young Lieutenant.

"The day is not over yet, sir." Gorski responded.

CHAPTER EIGHT

Raumschiff Twelve departed the docking area of the *Cleopatra* and was on its' way to the *Tonkin Gulf.* Flying the Raumschiff were Lieutenants Jason Allen and David French. There were only three passengers on the ship for the short trip. They were Dominic and two female Marine Corps Privates named Kappes and Taibbi. While they were on route, Dominic felt his personal holo-com vibrating which notified him of an incoming communication. Dominic excused himself from the company of the two Marine Corps women and walked down stairs to the storage rooms.

Dominic activated his holo-com and it revealed a three foot tall holographic view of Yuri Gorski standing in the stair well of the *Cleopatra.*

"Yuri," Dominic greeted his friend. "What is going

on?"

"Dom, are you alone" Gorski asked.

Dominic nodded, "Yes, I am. The pilots are up in the upper section. The two Marines are in the command room. What is going on?"

"We were attacked," Gorski informed him. "Doctor Macinlock is dead. All of the weapons officers and technicians are dead. The MI soldiers you captured are also dead. We lost almost all of our engineering staff as well."

"Is the situation contained? Do you need for me to return to the Cleopatra?" Dominic asked, his mind was racing with dozens of questions. "Who attacked?"

"Two people, Jerry Goodman and Anastasia Sikororsky. We took them out before they could do any more harm. Drew was injured in the fight, but not too badly. Listen, the Tonkin Gulf might not be safe. Shigeta wants us to only communicate on personal devices from now on and, most importantly, he wants you and your crew to very careful. What happened here just might be repeated on the Tonkin Gulf. Watch your back my friend. Harumi and Marco would be really cross with me if you don't come back to them."

Dominic laughed, "My friend my whole family would be on your ass. Remember my younger sisters,

Venus and Giola? You do not want them as enemies."

"Well, in that case I am glad they are members of the Gang to protect my little brother, Piotr." Gorski was laughing. He remembered the two girls well. Over the years the Gorski's, Andolini's and Evart's spent plenty of time together. All of Dominic's younger siblings called Yuri Gorski "Uncle Yuri." Gorski smiled at the fond memories he had of the entire Andolini clan. "I have to go. Things are happening over here. Be safe and contact me when you get to a secure location."

"Peace my friend," Dominic said as the image of Gorski disappeared. He placed his communication device back onto his utility belt. He stood for a few seconds, collecting his thoughts and then walked up to the second level of the space craft. Jason Allen had brought all of Dominic's belongings over when he had joined the mission. Dominic fished through the large foot locker with his uniforms and clothing. He found his tri-shot crossbow and some knives, throwing stars and his katana blade. He began strapping the weapons onto his web belt and the slots on the straps over his back and shoulders. If there was an ambush waiting for him on the *Tonkin Gulf*, he was going to be prepared to fight back.

Dominic rejoined the two Marines in the command area of the Raumschiff. The two women noticed that he had substantially added to his weaponry since they last saw him.

"Get ready," Dominic whispered to them. "Things might get a little rough on us over there on the Battle Cruiser. I was just informed that the majority of the crew of the Cleopatra were killed. We might be walking into an ambush."

Kappes and Taibbi began checking over their laser rifle and their laser pistols. The two women did not know Dominic well, but they had heard of his recent fight against several MI agents. The fact that Dominic was the type of officer that would stand up and fight against substantial odds was enough for them. They would follow his lead anywhere.

Captain Mara Sowa had been field promoted by Admiral Weems to take command of the U.N.S.C. *Tonkin Gulf*. She had been given a compliment of about one hundred additional crew members to assist her in flying the massive space ship to planet Cootron. Of the one hundred crew members she had several pilots and engineers at her disposal as well as weapons technicians and medical personnel. There were also two squads of Marines on board for security purposes. She also had her husband, Laurent Sowa, on board as the chief of the Medical Section.

Captain Sowa stood in front of the Captain's seat on the Command Station of the *Tonkin Gulf* as her communications officer notified her that Lieutenant Allen was bringing in Raumschiff Twelve to Docking Bay One. Sowa smiled and sat down at her seat. Allen and the other pilot, French, were experienced at their field. The two pilots currently on the Command Station of the *Tonkin Gulf* were new recruits holding the rank of Lieutenant Junior Grade and neither had ever flown a Battle Cruiser before.

Sowa looked over at the backs of their heads. They were both women from the Beijing Academy. They seemed capable enough. But having a pilot with experience would lower Sowa's stress level greatly.

Laurent Sowa sat back in his chair in the Medical Section. He had received the direction that they were to take the ship over. Sowa pulled out his back pack and looked over his shoulder to see if his nurses or the other doctor were watching him. They were too much into their personal conversation with each other to pay Sowa any attention.

Laurent pulled out a small black back pack and

reached inside. He found his foot long and foot and a half width old style laptop computer and laid it on the counter in front of him. He opened the lap top to reveal the typing keyboard and a screen. He looked over his shoulder at the other medical employees and noted they were still engaged in their personal interaction. He began typing in his passwords and saw the icon of the file he needed to access. He moved his mouse function to the icon and double clicked on it.

The screen displayed pictures of about twenty crew members. It was all of the individuals that Laurent Sowa had patiently trapped, sedated and then planted a mind control computer chip into their brains. The time had come to call them all to duty. One of the faces was his wife, Mara. He moved the mouse arrow to her face and double clicked on it. The computer put in a question in bold red letters asking: "ACTIVATE?" Below the question were two responses, for "YES" or "NO."

Laurent moved the mouse arrow over the answers and pressed "Yes." He then moved on to the next picture of Lieutenant Jake Brown and clicked on his photograph as well. Sowa took his time, activating each and every one of his soon to be "zombies" as he had referred to them. Alone, he would not be successful in taking the *Tonkin Gulf* and the *Cortez*. But with his army of controlled zombies, Laurent Sowa would soon have both of the Battle Cruiser's firmly under his control.

Laurent, who had taken the Hippocratic Oath to do no harm to others, calmly stood and pulled out a laser pistol from his black back pack. He carefully aimed at the doctor and four nurses that had been chatting it up for the last fifteen minutes. He then began pulling the trigger, methodically killing all five of them. He enjoyed shooting people in the mid-section since the shot normally would leave the victim suffering for a few minutes before they died. Sowa sat down in the center of the bodies and laughed as each one fought to stay alive and slowly died. He reveled in their cries of pain.

Mara Sowa felt unusually dizzy. She sat down in the Captain's chair and was breathing heavily. The entire room was spinning in circles. She felt hot flashes come over her body as she felt herself losing control of her mind. As fast as the dizziness came to her the feeling was gone. Mara Sowa realized that she was cognizant of everything around her and of her actions. But she could not stop herself.

Mara Sowa pulled out her laser pistol and killed the two Marine Corps women that were standing on guard duty on the Command Station. She turned and aimed at the weapons technician on the third balcony above and blew her head off with one shot.

The two Asian women sitting at the pilot and astral navigation seats died next as Mara Sowa shot them in the back of their heads. Their skulls exploded like watermelons being hit by a sledge hammer. The remaining technicians on the command station were not military service men or women. They were all civilians and they were all dead in less than twenty seconds. The bodies were strewn about the Command Station. Mara Sowa felt herself weeping at the fact she had just murdered members of her own crew. She had tried to stop herself from shooting all of them, but the powerful mind control device in her brain had overcome her free will. She fell to her knees, weeping uncontrollably and clutched her hands over her ears. She kept repeating the word "Why?" as she cried.

Unaware of the dangers on Level One, LaShondra Lewis was working her shift as the non-commissioned officer in charge of the Weapons Section on board the Battle Cruiser *Tonkin Gulf.* She was loading a laser battery charge into one of the laser canons that was secured to the east side of the section. She had a laser rifle slung over her left shoulder and a laser pistol and other weapons attached to her web belt. She watched as several civilian computer technicians worked to take inventory of the number of armor piercing rockets on board. Lewis had not allowed her mind to drift off into her personal problems with Harrison. She had resigned herself to the notion that she would deal with him in due time.

But now, duty called. They were all on alert for Defense Condition Four which meant they had to be battle ready. Lewis observed Commander Ervin Urbanczyk enter the weapons section followed by three Marines. Lewis' first inclination was to greet the Commander and give him a status report as to their military readiness. She was stunned when Urbanczyk and his three Marines pulled out laser pistols from their harnesses and began to open fire.

Lewis dived for cover behind a rack of ten six foot tall solar energy cells. She pulled her laser rifle from her shoulders and readied it for combat. She watched as several civilian technicians were blasted by laser fire from Urbanczyk and his Marines. They had been unarmed and killed in cold blood.

Lewis snarled and fired at the Commander and the Marines. Her first laser rifle shot hit one of the Marines in the lower torso, cutting the woman in half. Her second shot caught another female Marine in the chest, sending her body pieces splattering on the wall. Urbanczyk and the remaining Marine ran for cover, the Commander cursing as he ran. Urbanczyk had not anticipated any resistance, and certainly not from a person so well trained and accurate with a weapon. Lewis watched some of the civilian technicians had also scrambled for cover from the deadly onslaught.

Lewis worried that if the Commander and the other Marine fired upon the solar cells that she was hiding behind it could cause a massive explosion strong enough to destroy the outer hull and cause everyone in the second level of the Battle Cruiser to be swept out into space. Lewis quickly pulled out a thermite grenade, pressed the detonator and tossed it at Urbanczyk and his last Marine. She saw that Urbanczyk was diving for cover and the Marine was diving on top of the grenade.

Lewis used the temporary lull in the weapons fire to run from her hiding place and dive for the entrance to the Weapons Section. Her thermite grenade erupted to the pitiful screams of the Marine that had dived on top of it. Her body burned to ashes in seconds from the intense heat. Lewis stood behind the metal doorway and tried to get an open shot at Urbanczyk.

She could not locate him.

Several of the technicians that had survived the surprise attack ran toward Lewis, realizing that she was on their side. One by one they were able to make it to safety as Lewis kept her laser rifle aimed into the Weapons room. Wherever Urbanczyk was hiding, he was not coming out. Lewis counted each of the survivors as they ran past her, there were eight of them.

Urbanczyk sat behind a stockpile of protective metal casings that were stacked on the floor of the weapons room. The casings were dark green in color and each contained an R-5 armor piercing rocket inside. There were about fifty casings stacked in the form of a pyramid which offered Urbanczyk plenty of cover. He and his three Marines had not been ready for anyone to be quick enough on their feet to fight back. The woman in the black uniform was one sharp soldier. Urbanczyk wished that she were on his side and cursed Laurent for not getting a mind control implant in her brain. He gripped his laser pistol in his right hand and hoped that help would arrive soon.

Raumschiff Twelve arrived on the *Tonkin Gulf* without incident. Jason Allen landed the craft with competent ease and began shutting down the engines. As he descended the ladder leading up to the pilot section he was met by Dominic who handed him a laser rifle and pistol.

"What is this for?" Allen chuckled.

"Trouble," Dominic answered as he saw David French jump down onto the metal command area floor. Dominic handed him weapons as well.

"Something going on that we should know about?" French asked with hesitation in his voice as he took the weapons from Dominic.

"There was an attack on the Cleopatra. Doctor Macinlock and several others are dead. They were all ambushed by their own crew members." Dominic said, his voice low.

"And you expect that the same has occurred here?" Jason Allen asked.

"Absolutely. Don't you?" Dominic had his cross bow ready. "When we get out there, trust no one. Jason, when was the last time you communicated with the Command Station?"

"Just before we docked. Why?" Allen asked.

"Try them again," Dominic suggested.

Allen walked into the computer room and began trying to reach the command station.

"Look I happen to outrank all of you," French cut in. "You need to stand down Mister Military Intelligence." French pointed his index finger into Dominic's chest.

"Until I am told by Captain Sowa or Colonel Lincoln that there is a problem you can go fuck yourself."

Dominic slapped French's hand away from his chest. "I have solid intelligence that there is a reason for concern, sir. And if you touch me again, you will not have to worry about what waits for you outside. Your ass kicking will happen right here and now. Sir."

"You dare talk to a ranking officer in such a manner?" French demanded.

Allen cleared his throat, "Well, Lieutenant French, as I recall the regulations dictate that when involved in a land battle or a room clearing battle on a ship, which I think this falls into that latter category, the ranking Marine, Army or MI officer is in command. That means Second Lieutenant Andolini is in charge. I for one think we should follow his lead here. And he is right, no one is responding on the command station."

Allen had been briefed on the incident in which the landing party had been ambushed and Dominic single handedly took on the fight and won. Jason Allen felt more than comfortable following the Italian into combat. Allen also knew that French was an average officer at best and had been passed over for promotion to Lieutenant Commander three times. That normally meant there were some issues in the personnel file of David French.

"All right, Allen. All right." French said with an exasperated tone of voice as he shouldered the laser rifle and checked the charge on his laser pistol. "You want to follow this hothead into a danger zone? Then let's go. Andolini, you better not fuck up or so help me I will fire a shot into your backside."

Dominic did not comment on that last statement, believing it best to let it go for now. He led the two pilots down the stairs to the bottom receiving area for the Raumschiff and where the two Marines Kappes and Taibbi were waiting. The two women were fully armed, their laser rifles in their hands and numerous grenades and other combat devices stuffed in their harnesses and web belts.

"Sir, we scanned the outer area of the Docking Bay," Taibbi announced. "There are no hostile persons on level five."

"But we detected residue of laser fire on level one, two and three," Kappes reported. "Computer states that there are twenty-seven confirmed dead on board."

Dominic looked over at French, "Any questions, sir?"

French gritted his teeth, "My wife was on the Command Station. Her name is Nia French. Do we know if, if she was hurt?"

Dominic could see tears welling up in his eyes. He could see the pain of not knowing the fate of loved one written all over the face of the higher ranking officer. Dominic certainly sympathized with him due to the lack of information regarding his own wife Harumi. He put his free hand on French's shoulder. "Sir, we will try and get to your wife as soon as possible. But right now, I need you sir. I need all of us to go in there with clear heads. Do you follow me?"

French wiped the tears from his eyes and nodded. "I will be okay. Just get me to her as soon as possible."

"Yes sir," Dominic responded and pointed to French and Allen. "I need you two to bring up the rear. The Marines and I will take the lead. If anyone tries to take us from behind or flank us, do not hesitate to light them up."

"We're ready," Allen said as he slung the laser rifle over his shoulder. He had the laser pistol in his right hand as it had always been the weapon he was most comfortable with.

"Marines, move out. Slowly," Dominic ordered.

The five waited as the back door to the Raumschiff storage area slid open. The ramp slowly slid to the floor of the docking bay of the *Tonkin Gulf*. Before the ramp had completely touched the metallic floor, Kappes and Taibbi were already moving slowly down the ramp, aiming their laser rifles at the upper balconies of the docking bay. As the two women began to ascend the steps, Dominic followed them aiming his crossbow upwards and moving straight toward the closest set of stairs. French and Allen were last out of the Raumschiff, aiming their weapons as well. To the relief of all five, they made it to the third balcony landing without incident. Dominic motioned to the Marines to proceed toward the main hallway that connected the docking bay with some of the flight command offices, engines storage rooms and the all-important stair wells that would lead them up to the fourth floor and the engine room.

Lieutenant Jake Brown suddenly woke up from a deep sleep. He sat up and stood as if he were being controlled by some force. He wanted to sit back down, but he could not. His legs were moving toward his duffle bag and he knelt down before it and began unpacking his weapons and belongings. He located his large Marine issued knife, some thermite grenades, his laser pistols and laser rifle. He began to dress in his Marine Corps Class C uniform. His hands were trembling as he fought whatever was controlling him to no avail. In his mind was the command to kill everyone on the ship.

Brown laced his combat boots and gathered up his weapons into his web belt. He walked to the entrance of his sleeping quarters and was met by Doctor Laurent Sowa and ten Marines.

"Good morning Lieutenant," Doctor Sowa smiled. "We have work to do."

Brown fought the force in his brain, but he could not win that mental battle. "What kind of work?"

"The kind that begins in the engine room my dear Lieutenant," Sowa said. "Would you be so kind as to lead these ten Marines into battle and kill each and every sniveling person that you find there?"

Brown was shaking as he fought to break the control over his mind.

Sowa smiled and shook his head from left to right. "Please, Lieutenant. You cannot fight it. You simply must do as I say. Your mind belongs to me now. Kill the engineers. All of them and kill any and all that stand in your way."

"Yes sir," Brown struggled to say as he fought the control over his free will to no avail. He was dominated completely and could not fight the commands of Sowa. He felt his laser rifle in his hands. He motioned with his head toward the ten Marines. "Let's move!"

Brown followed the Marines to the stair well leading down to the fourth level of the *Tonkin Gulf*. Their boots were clanging on the metal stair case as the descended.

Laurent Sowa then turned and walked toward the elevator. He had to find out what was taking Urbanczyk so long in the weapons section. Something was amiss.

Brown and his Marines ran as fast as they could down the stairs. They were close to level Four and the exit for the Engine Room and the Life Support Control rooms when they heard an order to halt.

Dominic had taken a standing position at the Level Four stairwell exit, using the metal wall at the entrance as a shield to over half of his body and aimed a laser pistol at Brown and his team. "I said halt!"

Brown wanted to avoid a conflict with Dominic. Over the few months they had been on the *Cortez* together, they had become friends.

"Dominic, you need to move so we can get to the engine room!" Brown warned, struggling with the computer micro-chip in his brain. "Please! Move out of our way!"

"I will do no such thing!" Dominic responded sternly. He and Kappes had heard the footsteps running down the stairs at them. So, he ordered for Kappes, Taibbi, Allen and French to hide behind the walls so that whoever was coming would be lulled into thinking Dominic was alone. Dominic had ordered everyone to keep their weapons on stun function to avoid unnecessary casualties. The idea was to lure the group into a trap, knock them all unconscious and restrain them.

"Kill him!" One of the Marines screamed, unable to fight the implant in her brain any longer. The Marine pulled up her laser rifle in an attempt to fire upon Dominic.

Dominic regretted that he had to do what he had to. He pulled the trigger of his laser pistol and sent three shots into the group of Marines. Dominic then dived backward, into the hallway leading to the engine room, not waiting to see if his shots hit their targets. His aim was true. The Marine that was raising her laser rifle to fire on Dominic took two laser hits in her chest. Another Marine was hit in the left cheek. Both fell to the stair well, succumbing to the electrical charge from Dominic's expert laser fire.

The others charged down the stairs roaring with rage.

Dominic slid behind Taibbi who was kneeling with her laser pistol aimed at the stairwell entrance on the left side. On the right side of the entrance was Kappes, French and Allen. All three had their laser pistols ready. They had set the weapons to stun function as Dominic had instructed.

As the Marines charged out into the hallway, Dominic's small group began firing, cutting down the enemy as they entered their view point. The fight was over in seconds. Dominic counted eight Marines lying on the floor before them. He did not see Jake Brown.

"Jake!" Dominic bellowed. "Surrender to me and I will see to it that you are treated fairly. Please. There does not need to be any more violence here!"

"Dominic!" Brown's voice sounded tortured. "It is in my head! I can't fight it! Someone help me!"

"Everyone stand down," Dominic told the others. "Jake! I am coming in unarmed."

Dominic handed his laser weapon to Taibbi.

"No!" Brown's voice again. "I will kill you! I don't want to, but it is controlling me! Don't come in here!"

Dominic slowly stepped into the stairwell and saw Brown on his hands and knees, crying. He had a hand laser in his left hand that he was waiving around wildly, as if he were swatting at flies with the weapon. Brown looked up and his eyes met Dominic's.

"Jake, it's me, Dominic. Come with me and we can get you help. Please. I can get you some help."

Brown shook his head violently. "Who did this to me, Dom? Why? I can't fight it. It is making me kill."

"Give me your weapon, Jake." Dominic held out his hand toward the man.

Brown was shaking, as if he were shivering out in the freezing cold without clothing. His forehead and upper lip were covered with beads of perspiration. He slowly aimed his hand laser at Dominic. "I am sorry," Brown whispered.

Before Brown could pull the trigger, Jason Allen fired his own hand laser. Brown was hit by Allen's shot and he crumpled to the metal floor, unconscious.

"Thanks," Dominic took a breath of relief.

"No problem," Jason said as Kappes and Taibbi rushed in and cuffed and frisked Brown for weapons.

"Now what?" French demanded.

"I need you to stay here and secure the engine room." Dominic told French.

"But my wife is up in the command area!" French protested. "I need to get to her."

Dominic recovered his cross bow and began to shoulder it. "Yes, and you are far too emotional to be involved in a laser battle up there. What if they did this to your wife? Did you see that none of these Marines could control themselves? How would you be able to defend yourself or the rest of us, if she were under some form of mind control like Jake and the others? Stay here, sir. If your wife is up there we will find her."

French took in several breaths wondering how he would react if his wife was under some form of hypnosis or worse. He finally nodded his agreement. "Fine. I will secure the engine room. No one will get through the bulkheads."

"Good man," Dominic turned his attention toward Allen, Kappes and Taibbi. The two female Marines had removed all weapons from Brown and his team. Additionally they had cuffed them all in case they regained consciousness, assuring that they would not get far. Jason held a laser pistol in his right hand; his facial expression indicated that he had no fear of whatever they would encounter next. Confidant that each of his small group was mentally in the game, Dominic gave them a decisive order: "Let's move."

Dominic led the small team up the stair toward Level three and the medical area.

Laurent Sowa walked briskly down the western corridor leading to the weapons section. He heard some screaming and several footsteps running in his direction.

Sowa pulled out his hand laser and got down on one knee. He aimed toward the elbow turn in the hallway which was about thirty feet ahead of him. The footsteps grew closer and closer until he saw the escaping weapons technicians running around the corner.

Sowa cursed Urbanczyk. He had obviously failed. Sowa began firing his laser, severing limbs from the technicians and aiming for their abdomen area so they would all die painfully. He hit them all and stayed on the floor as he listened to their cries of pain.

Lewis also heard the cries from the fallen. She had sent the surviving technicians down the west hallway presumably to safety. Instead she had unwittingly sent them to their deaths. Lewis cursed at herself as she should have anticipated that Urbanczyk would not be alone. She felt horrible over the others being shot behind her.

Lewis decided she had to finish the melee and attempt to protect the civilians that were left, if any. She pulled out two concussion grenades from her web belt, pressed their detonator buttons and rolled them in the direction of Urbnaczyk's hiding place. She then turned to run back down the hallway toward the horrible cries of pain from those she had sought to protect. As she neared the turn in the hallway her grenades detonated. She used the explosions to cover the sounds of her footsteps and she charged down the turn in the hallway.

Laurent Sowa felt the explosion from the weapons room. The blast shook the floors and the walls vibrated. He stood up to steady himself and grabbed hold of the wall with his left hand. When the vibrations from the explosions ended, he heard some of the mortally wounded technicians still moaning in agony. Some were begging for death.

"Drop you weapon you son of a bitch!" LaShondra Lewis ordered. She had her laser rifle aimed at Sowa. She was only about ten feet away from him. She saw the technicians on the floor rolling in agony, some holding their mid-section and moaning. Lewis could tell the wounds were all fatal. "Only a Doctor would know how to shoot someone for maximum pain. You sick bastard!"

Sowa laughed at Lewis. He quickly sized her up. She was a mere Corporal which meant no college education.   Sowa determined he could talk Lewis into dropping her weapon by playing the race card with her. "Why are you so angry? Look at them. They are all Asian, white and Latino. You and I are the only black skinned people on this ship. You should be on my side. After the centuries of segregation and slavery our people endured. Remember the Racial Wars? When all of the other races stood by and allowed the Akarzdamedians to kill off the entire population on the African Continent? That is how the white people, the Asian and Hispanic people think of us. We are expendable, we exist to be used and tossed aside. You and I are the same! Our kind should stick together." Sowa paused for dramatic effect. "I know that you were with Harrison and I know that white woman stole him from you. That is what white people do to us. They divide us from each other. You and I are of the same race. No one else can understand us. Honey, we are the same."

Lewis heard the sounds of the men and women on the floor crying in agony. Most of their cries for help drowned out Sowa's self-serving speech.

"You know what Doctor?" Lewis snarled.

Sowa smiled back, certain that the woman would drop her weapon and join him. "What is that?"

"I am nothing like you," Lewis pulled the trigger to her laser rifle.

Laurent Sowa screamed when he realized he was going to die. The laser sliced into his neck, just below the jaw line. His head and neck exploded from the extreme heat of the laser. His headless body staggered and fell sideways to the ground.

Lewis spun around and faced the turn in the hallway

and saw no sign of Urbanczyk. The wounded continued to moan in pain.

Lewis reached into her utility belt, removed her holo-com and switched it on. "Medical? This is Corporal Lewis. Come in please. Is there anyone there?"

All she heard in return was static. She was certain that Sowa had killed all of the medical crew first. There was no one on the ship to help treat the wounded.

Lewis pulled out her laser pistol, switched the setting to kill and looked down at the wounded. She walked over to the dying, one at a time, and shot them in the chest to end their suffering. There were eight of them. Lewis sat down with her back against the wall when she was finished. She kept watch on the end of the elbow in the hallway for Urbanczyk and the tears of remorse flowed. She had to kill them to end their pain. It was a decision that she wished she had never been in a position to have to make.

After several minutes passed Lewis heard footsteps coming up the stairwell about thirty feet down the hall. She pulled out her laser rifle and prepared for another battle. She estimated that there must be four or five coming her direction. She waited as the sounds of the approaching steps grew closer. When she saw who it was she smiled.

"LaShondra!" Dominic yelled and ran to her.

She stood and accepted one of Dominic's customary bear hugs. She was crying on his shoulder. "Dom it was terrible. They are all dead."

"It's okay now. We are here. Were there any others?" Dominic asked her.

"There is one that I know of that is left in the weapons room. It is Urbanczyk. He ambushed us and I was the only one that had a chance to fight back. He is still in the weapons section." Lewis said as she wiped the tears from her eyes. "Doctor Sowa was one of them. He killed these people and I killed him."

Dominic looked over his shoulder toward Allen, Taibbi and Kappes. "You all know what we need to do?"

"Let's kill that son of a bitch," Allen said with a grimace on his face as he was looking over all of their dead crew mates. Before they had been called out to investigate the *Cleopatra* mystery, Allen had been ready to retire from the Space Command. Being a part of getting revenge for the innocents that had died made it worthwhile for Allen to stay in the service just a little while longer.

Taibbi and Kappes nodded in agreement. They were both moved to anger that so many of their fellow crew members had been slaughtered.

"Careful!" Lewis warned. "He could be anywhere."

Kappes and Taibbi took the point, moving slowly down the hallway to the weapons section. They slowly rounded the corner followed by Dominic, Allen and Lewis. The five made their way to the weapons area entrance and were surprised that they met with no resistance.

Allen followed Kappes to the right metal wall at the Weapons Section entrance. Taibbi, Lewis and Dominic took the left. With their backs hugging the wall and weapons in their hands they stayed silent, listening for any sounds.

It was silent.

"Commander!" Dominic finally yelled out. "This is Lieutenant Andolini of MI. The entrance is surrounded. Your attempt to take control of the ship has failed. If you surrender now I will take you in under my personal protection. I promise you will receive a fair trial. What say you?"

Urbanczyk was lying on the floor; each breath was a struggle for him. He was badly injured by the two grenades that Lewis had thrown into the weapons section. His left arm was torn from shrapnel. He left leg had suffered some cuts as well. He groaned and sat up, clutching a laser rifle in his right hand. He had already decided long before that he could not surrender. The rebels would use him like a trophy. They would put some of the newest forms of truth serum in his veins to get him to confess to all his family had done over the centuries to the rest of humanity. He would not let the lower classes of existence to use him in such a manner.

Urbanczyk stood up and aimed at the entrance with his rifle and began firing several bursts in the area where he had heard Dominic's voice. Dominic and Lewis dived to the floor as the laser blasts impacted the metallic wall that had been behind them. Allen was pushed backwards by Taibbi, for his own protection.

After Urbanczyk finished firing he laughed out loud. "That is my answer! Come and get me!"

Dominic feared that would be the response. He nodded to the others in the direction of their adversary. Kappes and Taibbi ran into the Weapons Section, firing their rifles. Dominic and Allen covered for them, firing from their position in a crisscross pattern. Kappes and Taibbi saw Urbanczyk firing in their direction. The two women slid and then crawled for cover behind some of the weapons stockpiles. Urbanczyk cursed and tried to run to his left toward the area where the command offices were located.

Jason Allen saw that the Commander was running

with a limp that favored his left leg. Allen took careful aim at the man and fired his hand laser. His blast hit Urbanczyk's left leg above the knee. Urbanczyk cried out and his body slid to the ground leaving his severed left leg kicking on the floor. As he fell, he lost his laser rifle which slid across the metal floor to the far wall and out of his reach.

Allen, Lewis and Dominic charged in as Urbanczyk attempted to crawl away. Kappes and Taibbi were joining in on the pursuit. Urbanczyk, sensing that he was about to be apprehended, rolled over on his back and pulled out his laser pistol. He raised the weapon to point it at the five soldiers charging at him. He was never able to pull the trigger. Dominic, Lewis and Allen opened fire at Commander Ervin Urbanczyk, riddling him with laser wounds. His body was torn to pieces.

The five stood over the remains of Urbanczyk for a moment.

"Now what?" Allen asked, breaking the uncomfortable silence.

"We take the Command Station," Dominic turned to Lewis. "Scan the upper level for life forms please and locate them."

Lewis went to one of the wall monitors and began

typing into the keypad under the monitor screen. She turned to the others. "Computer detects only one life form located on the Command Station."

"One of them?" Allen pointed at Urbanczyk's remains.

"Maybe," Dominic nodded. "Corporal Lewis, you are now commander of the Weapons Section. Wait here for further orders."

"But you might need me up there!" Lewis protested. After all of the death that she had witnessed she was not in the mood to be alone.

"I need you right here," Dominic told her calmly. "If this is all a beginning strike for a larger attack, then I need you here so this ship can fight back. I know you can handle the weapons area. Having you here will put my mind at ease."

Lewis stood at attention and saluted Dominic. He was her friend and he had proven to be a brave and smart officer. "Yes, Lieutenant."

He returned her salute.

Dominic led Kappes, Taibbi and Allen to the stair cases. The four ascended the stairs rapidly to arrive at the top level of the *Tonkin Gulf*. They ran past the many empty executive meeting rooms and quarters of the top command officers. They passed the large gymnasium and swimming pool. Next, they passed by the stellar cartography chambers. As they passed by each of the sections, they noted that there were no crew members present. The ship was eerily quiet.

The four stopped their run at the west entrance to the Command Station. The doors were open as opposed to shut as required by Space Command regulations.

Dominic, with his laser pistol drawn slowly stepped into the large rectangular shaped room. He saw the dead bodies of the two guards on the floor to his right and left. The two pilots were dead in their chairs, the top of their heads blown off. He saw several bodies hanging from the safety rails on the balconies above. He heard the sobbing from the Captain's chair. He ran to the sound of the crying.

He found Captain Mara Sowa, curled up in a fetal position and weeping like a child.

"Captain!" Dominic picked her up in his arms and shook her gently to gain her attention. She rolled her eyes at him and seemed to not be able to recognize him.

"Dominic!" Allen called from the pilot's section. "I found French's wife. She's dead. And the ship is set on a collision course with the Cortez."

"Can you avoid it?" Dominic handed Sowa over to

Private Kappes and then ran to Allen's side.

"Yeah, no problem." Allen moved the deceased pilots out of the seats for astral navigation and chief pilot. Allen sat down and began typing in commands and took the manual half-moon steering column in his hands to make the adjustments.

Captain Sowa was babbling about nothing coherent and was staring at the far wall. It was as if she had lost her mind.

"Frisk her and cuff her," Dominic said with sadness in his voice. "She could still be a danger."

"Yes sir," Taibbi responded.

Dominic pulled out his private hand held communication device. "Computer, patch me in to a one on one conversation with Lieutenant Yuri Gorski."

He waited for a few moments until Gorski's image appeared before him. "Dominic! Thank the Stars! What is going on over there?" Gorski asked.

Dominic shook his head slowly, "Nothing good, my friend. Computer confirms that there are only twenty of us left alive. We were hit very badly, Yuri. Captain Sowa is in a catatonic state. Doctor Sowa is dead as is Commander Urbanczyk. Lieutenant Brown is out of commission. There are only eight of us left to operate the Battle Cruiser."

"Do you have any pilots?" Gorski asked.

"Two," Dominic answered. "And we have three engineers, three enlisted women and myself. Everyone else is either dead or under arrest."

Gorski shook his head in disbelief. The entire mission had exacted a large toll in lives lost. "Are you okay?"

Dominic nodded slowly, thinking of David French waiting for news of his wife. "Tell me, how do I tell a man that his wife is dead?"

Gorski looked down at his feet, wondering how his father had felt all those years ago when he was told of how his wife had died. "I have no clue how to answer that question. Dom, we received a news report from the broadcasts of old Earth. Nevada Territory and Ireland declared independence. There are rebellions starting all over the eight solar systems. Thousands of people marched on the United Nations Building of planet New Quebec and the soldiers allowed them to take it without a fight. The Royal Family members there were taken prisoner. There are people rising up on the Martian Colonies. We also heard from Admiral Khan's Fleet."

Dominic grew quiet. His twin brother, Marco, was serving on that Fleet as a fighter pilot. Dominic had thought he had lost his brother once before, during the Blood Moon Incident. He prepared himself for the worst. "What happened, Yuri?"

Gorski cleared his throat. "It would seem that Admiral Khan and his Fleet are challenging the Glorious Leader. Khan issued an ultimatum for Vladimir Sikorsky to surrender himself for prosecution."

"How did that go over?"

"Sikorsky declared Khan and all of his Fleet enemies of the United Nations and the Space Command," Gorski said softly. "Sikorsky ordered that the Fleet be annihilated. None of the Second Fleet will be allowed to surrender. Prisoners will not be accepted. I am sorry, Dom."

"Marco is not dead yet. I think our Glorious Leader is turning more and more people against him with these draconian measures."

"Tell me about it," Gorski agreed.

CHAPTER NINE

Planet Cootron was a virtual paradise when first conquered by humanity. The atmosphere was just like that of planet Earth. Cootron had green fields, edible plant life, huge trees, smaller trees, hills, mountains, plains, wetlands, water covering approximately seventy percent of the surface and indigenous life forms that were, for the most part, non-poisonous. Although there were some lethal creatures on the planet, humanity was able to take the planet by force, colonize her and begin building for the influx of immigration to come in the future. The original settlers had pushed to name the planet New Earth, but that was not approved by the Glorious Leader. The Sikorsky family named the planet Cootron after the astronaut that first landed there, Captain Coolidge Tron Franklin, using part of his first name and his middle name.

Over the years, the Sikorsky's had placed one of their own to manage the day to day business of the planet. Cootron Governor Vladimir Sikorsky, IV, had been the civilian leader of the entire planet for the past twenty years. Although he was the great grandson of the Glorious Leader, the position was not easy. This was not a job for a lazy person. Governor Sikorsky normally worked ten hours per day to ensure that the daily needs of the planet and her inhabitants were met.

Serving under Governor Sikorsky were a General of the Military Intelligence, a General of the Marines, an Admiral of the Space Command and a General of the Armed Forces Security branch. Each of these four high ranking military service members were great grandchildren of the Glorious Leader. They ruled the planet with an iron fist, controlling brigades of soldiers and pilots that were sworn to die in their service. The MI branch was referred to as the Gestapo by the citizens of Cootron. Freedom was limited as Governor Sikorsky had implemented planet wide curfews and other laws against political free speech and weapons ownership.

In addition to overseeing the military, Governor Sikorsky was in charge of the infamous Cootron Prison, which took up an entire continent. The Warden of the prison was Governor Sikorsky's daughter, Stacia Sikorsky. The prison was the largest in the Earth Empire and received prison transport ships from all of the other planets, sometimes on a daily basis, to house the violent criminals to those that spoke out against the Glorious Leader. Under Warden Stacia Sikorsky's management, many criminals vanished. She would locate young women that had been convicted and have them removed to an island nearby the Prison Continent so that surgeons for the Royal Family could determine whether the internal organs of the prisoners were worthy of harvesting for transplants. Stacia, her siblings and their children and her father all took advantage of remaining young through the forced contributions of the female prison population.

Governor Vladimir Sikorsky IV had twelve wives, many more lovers on the side and ninety-one children. His grandchildren numbered over three hundred. He used his position to provide his descendants with great careers and excellent salaries.

In essence, all of the best paying employment on Cootron was taken by a Sikorsky. The positions of power were also under the Royal Family control. Any that spoke out against them ended up as an invited guest to the Prison

Continent, which was eventually a death sentence.

But the reign of Governor Sikorsky, IV, was about to come to an abrupt ending.

The family did not give a second thought to the arrival of three Battle Cruisers in orbit around Cootron. The military and the Space Command understood that Cootron and her three Space Stations and two moons were all natural destinations for space vessels to obtain supplies, transfer passengers and take care of other forms of commerce. The three Battle Cruisers had escorted approximately one dozen large civilian transport space craft, several hundred Raumschiff's and about two thousand five hundred small Allen Type fighter craft.

Admiral Alejandro Cardenas had a hole in his heart. He had lost his son, Porfirio, on the Blood Moon Incident. The death of his beloved son would have pushed the Admiral into depression and despair had it not been for a surprise visit from Penelope. She showed Cardenas evidence that the Royal Family had assisted in the ambush of Porfirio Cardenas and his fellow cadets. Penelope used video, computer recordings, documents and photo imaging to plead her case to the grieving Admiral that the Royal Family must be overthrown.

Cardenas, after carefully reviewing the proof

presented by Rosenburg determined that she was correct. The Glorious Leader must be removed from power. His two hundred year reign of terror must come to an end.

Admiral Cardenas, in his pain and despair, turned his depression into purpose. He joined the small rebellion led by Penelope Rosenburg. Together, they carefully recruited crew members from the Cleopatra, the Tonkin Gulf and the other three Battle Cruisers under Cardenas command. Cardenas learned from Penelope that his ships were infested with several dozen Sikorsky descendants that were absolutely loyal to the Glorious Leader. Cardenas agreed that all of the Royal Family members on his space crafts must be eliminated.

To the dismay of Cardenas, all five of his Captains were from the Sikorsky lineage. Killing them all would not be easy. Innocent crew members were loyal to their Captain and would fight to the death for them. This blind loyalty had to be neutralized to avoid losing good pilots and soldiers in the purge.

Penelope supplied Cardenas with loyal soldiers to assist in removing the Royal Family members that were crew men and women on the Battle Cruisers. Cardenas was amazed that the soldiers that worked with Penelope Rosenburg were all clones, duplicates, of several men that had died. One of the sets of clones was called Drayton Love-Easter and wore printed numbers on their left shoulder sleeves to give some semblance of identification between them. Another set of clones were all named Garrison and each had a different first name to differentiate them from the other. Each of these copies or clones had the memories of the original Drayton Love-Easter and the original Lieutenant Garrison. They each also had computerized downloads into their brains of military tactics, weapons and self-defense. But, after the process to create them had been completed, they each created their own, separate memories.

The third set of clones was of a woman named Ella Ragnarsson, who, according to Penelope, had been a master assassin. The Ella clones were given the memories and knowledge of Penelope as opposed to the recollections of the Ragnarsson woman. Penelope had explained that it would have been a dangerous proposition to have the memories of Ella Ragnarsson since she had been loyal to the Sikorsky Regime. The Ella clones, with the memories of Penelope, also had additional digitized knowledge downloaded for weapons proficiency, martial arts, military tactics, piloting skills and world history.

The battle to free the five heavily armed Battle

Cruisers from the Sikorsky installed officers corps was hard fought. Admiral Cardenas, with the assistance of acclaimed Astro-biologist and medical doctor William Wakefield, were able to use DNA scans to determine who the Sikorsky's were versus those that were not. Wakefield gave the technology to make the identification scans much easier and precise to Penelope Rosenburg and the crew of her Raumschiff called the Peacemaker. As the battle began, Cardenas, Wakefield and the duplicate Garrison's, Love-Easter's and Ella Ragnarsson's discovered that many crew members had been operated on and inside their brains were complex and advanced micro-chips which were utilized to control their minds by the Sikorsky crew members. To make matters worse, each of the Sikorsky members had been given specialized weapons by the Glorious Leader to be used in case they were ever attacked.

These vicious new weapons were in the form and shape of a laser rifle, but they fired a new and deadly form of projectile. These weapons targeted human bone structure and the force of the weapon beam would crush a person's entire bone formation into liquefied powder. The result was a painful death and a puddle of flesh and internal organs littered all over the five ships. Most of the victims had been some of the duplicates of Love-Easter, Garrison and Ella.

The battle to take the Cleopatra became costly in lives. Captain al-Bashir had numerous Marines under his control with brain implanted micro-chips. It was only that Captain al-Bashir let his guard down that ended his life. One of his own wives, Rima al-Bashir executed her husband by decapitating him. Unfortunately, there were too many of the Sikorsky controlled Marines on the *Cleopatra* and the Tonkin Gulf to continue the fight. Admiral Cardenas ordered that each of the forces loyal to the rebellion to disengage the face to face combat and to disable the engine rooms.

The act left the two Battle Cruisers floating in space with a small compliment of Sikorsky loyalists on board. Those loyal to Cardenas escaped in Raumschiff's to board the other three Battle Cruisers, the *New Hampshire*, *British Columbia* and *Stirling Bridge*.

The many civilian transport ships that were being escorted by the five Battle Cruisers also became involved in the battle. On one of the Transports was a retired Marine Corps General named Kenneth Charles Knox, called "KC" by his friends. Knox had been planning on living out his years on planet Cootron at a ranch he had purchased. He, his several wives and children planned on raising livestock and making a living as ranchers. Knox had been a war hero several times over and was instrumental in assisting Admiral Cardenas in winning the majority of the Transport ships over to the side of the anti-Sikorsky forces.

After the battle was won, Penelope departed in her Raumschiff the Peacemaker to take the fight to several of the science vessels in the far reaches of space. Cardenas, Knox, Rima al-Bashir, Doctor Wakefield, the surviving officers and duplicates of Garrison, Love-Easter and Ella Ragnarsson devised their plans to conquer planet Cootron.

Cardenas and Knox devised an attack that would be fought in ten different locations, each attack synchronized to begin simultaneously. The moon bases, the space stations and the military strongholds had to be taken quickly. Once the element of surprise was lost, the Sikorsky controlled planet would be able to annihilate the three Battle Cruisers with the nuclear arsenal which was controlled in the Military Intelligence buildings nearby the capital. Knox directed a company of the cloned soldiers and some Marines be sent in to either destroy or occupy the Military Intelligence building. They would ignite an explosion once they were successful in their task. The explosion would be the signal for all of the other attacks to begin.

Admiral Cardenas dispatched several Raumschiff's

to transport platoons of Marines and cloned Love-Easter's, Garrison's and Ella Ragnarsson's to the moon s and space stations. Their mission was to take the engine rooms and life support areas. The Battle Cruisers would fire upon the weapons stations when the signal was given.

The Raumschiffs had landed on the moons orbiting planet Cootron as planned. The passengers of the Raumschiff space crafts were dressed as tourists, soldiers on leave and business men and women. But the stated purpose of each of the Raumschiff occupants was a ruse. Each of the new visitors of the Moon bases was sent by their commanding officer, Cardenas, for a specific purpose. As the numerous crew members of Cardenas crew milled around the lunar buildings, acting as tourists and shoppers, their real goal was to seize control of the lunar bases at a specified hour, minute and second.

Similar groups had been dispatched by the Admiral to occupy the space stations orbiting Cootron so that they could be in position to wrest control of those massive man-made structures when the time for the invasion began.

Cardenas left nothing to chance. He was well aware of the offensive and defensive capabilities of the military presence on both the lunar bases and the space stations. Any successful attack on planet Cootron required that the aggressor take immediate control of those facilities.

The morning of December twentieth seemed to start like any other day. Governor Sikorsky and a few of his wives, children and grandchildren had breakfast as they did any other day. The Governor's mansion was located in Sikorsky City and stood some eighty floors high. The top ten floors were used as sleeping quarters for the Governor and his family. Each of the top ten floors had large balconies that were capable of seating about one hundred people comfortably around the several oval shaped tables. In the distance were the beautiful views of the Cootron Mountain Range, several picturesque waterfalls and rolling hills. The mountains were covered with snow and the citizens of Cootron enjoyed skiing the mountains.

Governor Sikorsky loved drinking his coffee from the balcony on the eightieth floor, watching the wonders of this spectacular planet and her population of humans. The staff of slave Akardamedian's brought the Sikorsky family their food and drinks which consisted of scrambled eggs, steaks, and a form of grilled nopal that was indigenous to Cootron, breads, toast, fruits, coffee, juices and water.

As the family members were being served, one of the grand children, a beautiful thirty year old woman named Skye Sikorsky was standing at the rails at the edge of the balcony. Her blonde hair was blowing in the wind. She was one of the few Sikorsky's that had refused to accept body parts from others to keep herself alive. Part of the reason she had not done so was that she was still very young and attractive in her own right. The other was that Skye Sikorsky had secretly listened to some of the live broadcasts of Pastor Love-Easter. Through his teachings, Skye Sikorsky had embraced a life as a Christian, which was against her family teachings and desires. To keep her acceptance of Christ from her family, she tattooed the sign of the cross on her lower back, not on her face as Pastor Love-Easter taught. Skye Sikorksy had studied astro-biology in school and had earned a doctorate in that field. She was currently a Professor at the Science Department for one of the many universities on Cootron.

Skye Sikorsky squinted her blue eyes and stared off into the distance. She looked over the massive space craft landing field below and the fifteen floor Military Intelligence building to the east. She thought she saw an eruption on the rooftop of the MI Building, a ball of fire that was orange, red and yellow. She turned to her family who were all beginning to sit down to enjoy their meal.

"I think there is a fire down in the military command building," Skye announced to the others.

"I am certain there are just some weapons tests going on." Vladimir Sikorsky, IV, waived his hand as if to dismiss the subject. "Come, sit down and eat."

"But it looked bad," Skye Sikorsky told them as she walked toward the Governor. She stopped in her tracks, feeling as if something had stung her in the back of her neck. Skye instinctively reached back with her left hand and felt something sticking out of the back of her neck. It felt like a thin piece of plastic. She pulled it out and looked at it for a moment. It was a dart. She realized she had been hit by a stun dart as her surroundings began to spin in circles. Before Skye Sikorsky could cry out to warn her family, she collapsed to the granite tiled balcony, unable to move.

Three dozen men and women, flying with the assistance of Brackenridge Corporation metal flight rockets strapped to their backs, ascended to the eightieth floor of the Governor's building. The flight packs were powerful enough to fly a person of up to five hundred pounds in weight. Each of the attackers was wearing black helmets and black uniforms. They each were holding laser pistols in their hands. The Governor and his family did not notice as they silently hovered over the brick balcony wall. The ambush was flawless. Cardenas, who was the leader of this part of the battle, opened fire with the hand lasers in his hands, spraying the balcony with red colored beams. General Knox, Rima al-Bashir and several Love-Easter clones did the same, carefully aiming at their targets and firing their hand lasers. The Governor and his family members were all hit with blasts and fell to the granite floor. It was over in seconds.

Alejandro Cardenas landed onto the roof and turned off his metal rocket glider pack. He removed his helmet, pulled out a hand held communication device and activated it. "This is Admiral Cardenas. We have secured the Governor's mansion. Team two has taken out the Military Intelligence building. Take out the defenses as planned."

"Yes sir," came the response.

The bombardment was brutal and deadly. The barracks at the military space craft landing strips were hit by guided rockets fired by diving Allen Type space craft. Thousands of pilots were vaporized in seconds. Cardenas pilots assured that their attack did not damage any of the valuable space craft that were on the landing strips. They only targeted the military areas to eliminate the soldiers that were known to be completely loyal to the Sikorsky's.

Next, one of the three Battle Cruisers in orbit began to descend into the atmosphere, on an intercept course with the prison continent. The other two Battle Cruisers began to fire their canons and armor piercing rockets at the lunar surfaces and weapons areas of the space stations. The military out posts on the moons of Cootron were hit and destroyed. The soldiers in those posts were either killed in the blasts or when they were swept out into space from the explosive decompression.

The space stations were hit in their weapons sections only. In seconds, each space station was left defenseless from the surprise attack of Admiral Cardenas' two Battle Cruisers. As the rocket and laser attacks from the battle cruisers commenced, the planted soldiers on the space stations moved with precision and took the engine control rooms and life support facilities without incident. The technicians and engineers all surrendered without a fight.

The main military base on Cootron was strafed several times by Raumschiffs and small Allen type fighter ships. The soldiers on the planet surface tried in vain to fight back, their bodies exploding when struck by the deadly laser blasts. Thousands died in a matter of sixty seconds.

The surviving Marines, MI, Pilots and Army soldiers scattered from their burning buildings and bunkers. They were firing laser pistols and rifles at the attacking space craft. The pilots on board the attacking Raumschiffs and small fighter craft began to fire back on them. Another thousand Cootron defenders were obliterated. Only two of the Admiral's small fighter ships were shot down in the short and decisive battle.

The rest of the soldiers on the surface of planet Cootron threw down their weapons and held up their arms, hoping their attackers would take prisoners. Cardenas had already instructed his pilots to cease the attack once the ground troops surrendered.

Cardenas watched as his fellow gliders began checking on the unconscious men and women on the granite tiled floor of the Governor's mansion. They identified each and every person as either a Sikorsky or a spouse of a Sikorsky.

"Wake them up," Cardenas said to his longtime friend, Doctor William Wakefield.

Wakefield had been serving with Cardenas for about a decade, first when Cardenas was a Captain and continuing on when the position as Admiral came about. Wakefield was a man of scientific knowledge and had earned several awards for his research, lecture tours and publishing. He was in his fifties, had several wives and children and completely loyal to Cardenas.

Retired General Knox of the Marine Corps was also on the roof top with them. He had been close friends to the Admiral for many years. He had been a hero of the Dinosaur wars on planet New Edinburgh and had led Marines into battle on planets Athena, New Vladivostok and New Berlin. Knox had grown weary of the Sikorsky rule of humanity many years ago when the regime ordered the slaughter of Marines under his command that had been sent to investigate a derelict alien space craft. One of the dead was a Lieutenant named Melita Gorski. In the Dinosaur Wars, Knox became close friends to the widowed husband, Nikolai Gorski. Knox always felt guilt in his heart that he did not speak up more to save the men and women under his command those many years ago. By joining Cardenas, he had a chance to end the dictatorship of Vladimir Sikorsky, or die trying.

Rima Chancellor al-Bashir was a lovely brunette that had been the youngest wife to Captain Faisal al-Bashir of the *Cleopatra*. When the battle to take the Fleet began, Rima al-Bashir chose to help Cardenas against her abusive husband. She took pleasure in being the one that decapitated Captain al-Bashir before the *Cleopatra* was abandoned.

The rest of the team on the rooftop were duplicates of Ella Ragnarsson (who went by the name Penella), Frank Garrison and Drayton Love-Easter. They had been left by Penelope Rosenburg with Cardenas to assist in the hostile takeover of planet Cootron.

When Penelope first approached Cardenas on board the *Cleopatra*, he was grief stricken by the death of his son, Porfirio. When she revealed her evidence against the Sikorsky's to Cardenas and explained her intention to over throw the Sikorsky regime, Cardenas had been skeptical. Cardenas did not believe it could be done.

Now, Cardenas was a believer. He was able to enlist the aid of the majority of his crew that was not related to the Glorious Leader. His co-conspirators were able to kill almost all of the Sikorsky plants on his five Battle Cruisers, less a few that were using special alien technology to hide on board the *Tonkin Gulf* and the *Cleopatra*. The decision was made to take all of the surviving personnel to the other three Battle Cruisers and disable the *Cleopatra* and *Tonkin Gulf*. Penelope had left with Cardenas all of the military intelligence he needed to mount a lightening attack on the Sikorsky forces. Cardenas, Knox, Wakefield and Rima al-

Bashir developed the plans. It had been decided that they would take out the MI headquarters first, then hit the Governor's mansion as the family had their morning breakfast, then wipe out the lunar bases with military functions and the weapons sections of the space stations. While this was occurring, simultaneous attacks on the pilots and Marines on the planet surface would take place.

The secondary attack would soon begin, to liberate the falsely accused prisoners on the southern continent of the planet.

Cardenas looked at each of the Sikorsky family members that were now sitting in chairs, hand cuffed and their feet tied with plastic twist ties.

"You will all die for this!" Vladimir Sikorsky, IV raged. His face red was with anger. "My father, his father and the Glorious Leader will hunt you down to kill all of you! This is an outrage! What gives you the right?"

Cardenas was about to answer when several more clones of Ragnarsson, Garrison and Love-Easter arrived, dragging with them the Sikorsky family Generals and Admirals that were living in the mansion. The search of the building had been completed in less than fifteen minutes of the first attack. The Generals and Admirals were also wearing restraints and were forced to sit on the granite floor of the balcony.

Cardenas pursed his lips and stood before Sikorsky, IV, and the other Generals and Admirals. "I have the right because our creator endowed us all with the right to liberty. You see, your family caused my son to be murdered. Now, it is time for you each to answer for your sins."

"Admiral, we found a dungeon in the basement levels." One of the Penella clones told him. "They had a few dozen young girls, around the ages of sixteen to twenty-two. They were all slated to be cut open for their internal organs."

"We released them all and killed their guards," Drayton Love-Easter #122 informed the group. "The girls followed us up to the eightieth floor, but we told them to wait inside. We did not think it would be a good idea for them to see the executions."

Cardenas nodded to the others. Knox, al-Bashir, the Garrison clones and Love-Easter clones each pulled out short swords from their sheaths that were strapped to their left legs.

Cardenas had his sword in his hands and walked to Vladimir Sikorsky, IV and stood inches from his face. "How many innocents died to give your body parts to make you immortal? How many others did you order killed to maintain your obscene power?"

"I am a Sikorsky. I am a god among men. I am immortal. The rest of you are just lab rats to us." Sikorsky, IV, was now screaming at the men and women with Cardenas. Even in restraints he was defiant and unapologetic for his crimes. "You should be glad that we allowed you to live as long as you have. Those bitches in the basement cells, they were blessed to be chosen to donate their livers, spleens, kidneys, hearts, lungs, skin, eyes and hair to the Sikorsky's. Being chosen to have their internal organs harvested for my family was an honor!"

Skye Sikorsky was also tied up and unable to move due to the stun dart that had been used against her. She cleared her throat and realized she still had use of her voice. She had an uneasy feeling that she and all of her family were about to die. She watched in horror as Cardenas shoved his sword into the chest of Vladimir Sikorsky, IV. He quickly yanked the sword out of Sikorsky's chest and then swung it down in an arc and severed his head from his body. All of the Sikorsky family members began to scream and cry. Some begged for mercy as Cardenas picked up Governor Sikorsky's head by the hair and showed it to all of them.

The Generals and Admirals were next. Knox

decapitated an Admiral as Rima al-Bashir did the same to a General. The multiple Love-Easters also took part in the beheading of the General officers. The Garrison and Ragnarsson duplicates did the same. There were about fifty Sikorsky's dead in under a few minutes. Their severed heads were being collected into bags.

Cardenas turned his attention to the spouses of the Sikorsky's, their children, their spouses and their children. Skye Sikorsky was weeping as she listened to what the man had to say. She knew she was about to die as the others.

"The rest of you will be tested," Cardenas told them. "If you are a descendant of the Glorious Leader, you just might die. Your death will be quick, I promise you. Some of you may survive the day. I am sorry, but the seed of the Glorious Leader must be eliminated."

Skye Sikorsky wanted to scream when the man named Wakefield scanned her. She saw Wakefield nod to one of the Love-Easter clones. "Her DNA is a Sikorsky; move her over to the group to be executed."

Drayton Love-Easter #99 lifted Skye Sikorsky in his muscular arms and carried her to a growing group of other descendants of the Glorious Leader. Many were crying and begging for their lives. Their pleas for mercy fell on deaf ears; their captors were true believers in their mission to wipe out the entire Sikorsky genealogy. As Love-Easter #99 sat Skye Sikorsky down he saw that her blouse was lifted and the small of her back and stomach were exposed. Love-Easter #99 noticed the mark of the cross on her back.

"I think we might have one here worth saving." Love-Easter #99 announced suddenly.

Wakefield walked over to where Skye Sikorsky was lying on the granite and scanned her with a different instrument. "She has had no body parts added to her with differing DNA. That alone is different from all the others. But she is a Sikorsky."

"She has the sign of the cross on her body," Love-Easter #99 told the others. "I think we ought to allow her to plead her case after the stun dart poison wears off."

Cardenas nodded, "Fine, we will give her a chance then since she is the only one here that has not stolen body parts from other people. She lives for now. Kill all the others."

The other Sikorsky's were screaming as the group began decapitating them, one by one. The screams were over after several minutes. Blood covered the cobblestone balcony.

Cardenas looked to the now widowed spouses and

the new born babies. "You were the wives and husbands of the despots that lie dead. You will now choose, do you live or die like they did. Your choice for life means that you will side with us in our war to overthrow the Glorious Leader."

"Before you answer the question put to you, consider this point." Rima al-Bashir said, walking in front of the crying group of widows. "I was just like you. I was married to a Royal. I joined Admiral Cardenas and General Knox because it was the right thing to do. I killed my own husband and was glad to do it. If you join us, you will probably have to kill many more Sikorsky's. We estimate that the Sikorsky clan numbers in the five hundred thousand range. There is plenty of killing to be done. You may be angry that we just killed your husbands and wives. But they did not love you. Doctor Wakefield will now conduct more scans on each of you to see if your spouses had computer chips implanted in your brains to control you. The Sikorsky's have been known to commit this act. My dead husband had done it to me."

Wakefield was running yet another hand held scanning device by each of the spouses. About ninety percent of them had microchips in their heads. Wakefield announced the results to Cardenas and the others.

"After we operate and remove the computer devices from your brains, you will regain your free will," Cardenas told them. He understood all too well how overwhelming the events had been for the widows. Their entire world had just been flipped upside down in a matter of minutes. He then ordered for the widows that required surgery to be removed to another location. For the ten percent that did not have a mind control device in their brains, their time had come.

It was time for them to pick who they would stand with in the revolution.

The third Battle Cruiser, the UNSC *Sterling Bridge*, had neared its destination of the Prison Continent. The dreaded Cootron Prison was the last stop for many convicted criminals that were sentenced to death. At the infamous prison facility, those with the death sentence were killed in the manner that they had inflicted death. If their underlying crime had not resulted in the death of another, the convicted felon was generally executed in some gruesome way. Many were barbequed alive, and then eaten by prisoners that were ravenous with hunger. Women were raped and beaten to death. Some were drowned in acid. Others were sent to die in one of the many arenas on Cootron to the applause of the masses. Gladiatorial warfare on Cootron was barbaric and vicious.

Ancient Rome was tame compared to the ways prisoners were killed on Cootron.

Sadly, many of the condemned were convicted for conspiracy against the Royal Family which was a death penalty offense. Those prisoners were always sent to die in one of the arenas.

The prison occupied an entire continent on planet Cootron. The two hundred foot high walls around the main command buildings existed to keep the jail employees segregated from the prison population.

The continent was surrounded by water which was populated by giant meat eating aquatic life. Prisoners that attempted to build a boat out of tree wood were generally devoured by the indigenous, giant, water breathing creatures. Even with that danger, many prisoners attempted to escape by way of sea and either died as a meal or from exposure to the sunlight as they sailed aimlessly in the ocean.

Many of the prisoners resorted to cannibalism to survive. It was not uncommon for parents to eat their children or for spouses to kill one another in their sleep and then dine on their raw flesh.

Warden Stacia Sikorsky was married to her brother

and they had created several children together. Her brother had twelve wives and many offspring from them as well. All of their family lived on the Prison Continent, segregated from the condemned that had been deposited to the area and quickly forgotten by all.

On the command station of the *Stirling Bridge* was Commander Zarko Radmonovic, a giant of a man at seven feet five inches tall. He had been the executive officer of the ship when the purge of all of the Sikorsky descendants occurred. Radmonovic was field promoted to Captain the *Stirling Bridge* until further notice. He ordered his pilot to come to a complete stop over the main offices of the Prison Continent. He ordered his communications technician to patch him into the Warden.

"Warden Stacia Sikorsky. This is acting Captain Radmonovic of the Battle Cruiser Stirling Bridge. A matter of national security has arisen. The entire planet is under siege. I need for you and your staff to board my personal Raumschiff so that we may get you to safety. Do you understand?"

"Why should I trust you?" Stacia Sikorsky replied.

"Because all of your family members are being executed," Radmonovic read from the hand written script given to him by Admiral Cardenas. "You can attempt to verify for yourself, but I can only defend this location for a few more moments."

The main prison control offices were about ten square miles in land space. Many of the buildings were as high as fifty floors up. Stacia cut off the communication with the Battle Cruiser *Stirling Bridge* and began attempting to communicate with her family at the Governor's palace. She received no response. She then tried to raise her relatives on the moon bases and space stations. Again, no response. She attempted the MI building to raise her brother who was the commanding General there. And there was no answer.

Stacia bit her bottom lip and turned to her six adult cousins, three adult daughters and one adult son and motioned for them follow her. She asked her computer satellites to show views of the planet Cootron. She and her family members saw the destruction of the military installations and the many body parts of soldiers scattered here and there. Then she had her computer satellite system scan the moons and space stations. The carnage was evident to her. They were virtually alone against an unknown enemy.

"Captain Radmonovic, we gratefully accept your offer of protection." Stacia told him. "We are coming out."

Stacia led out of the offices another sixty-seven Sikorsky family members, including her husband. They fled as fast as possible to get out of the building, expecting an attack at any moment. When they exited the structure, the saw a dozen Raumschiff space craft on the ground with many Empire soldiers securing the area.

Stacia smiled, believing the soldiers were her angels of mercy when in reality they were to become her executioners.

The soldiers began firing laser rifles on the Sikorsky's. Their bodies were blasted to chunks of flesh and meat as the snipers cut them down. Stacia screamed in fear and tried to run just before her upper torso was blown to a thousand pieces. Her husband was slashed in two when a laser blast hit him in the lower abdomen. The children of Stacia Sikorsky also fell in the rain of laser fire. The execution of the Warden and her staff took little time to complete.

The soldiers of the *Stirling Bridge* moved in to secure the Prison Control areas. The domination of planet Cootron had taken less than an hour. Only two pilots under Admiral Cardenas command lost their lives in the battle.

All of the adult Sikorsky family members on the surface, the moons and space stations were dead, all save the one named Skye.

"The long flight to liberate Cootron from tyranny had been worthy." Cardenas told his team on the roof of the Governor's mansion. "KC, you are now the Governor of planet Cootron. I trust you will offer the people freedom."

Knox nodded, "Of course. Should we address the civilian population? If they do not get information about the coups there could be widespread panic."

Cardenas nodded thoughtfully, "You are correct my friend. Let's send out a press release to the good people of Cootron. Their days of living in fear are over."

"Now, we can wait for the next round of fighting to begin. Soon, we will have to take this war to Sikorsky's Planet." Rima al-Bashir reminded the men.

Doctor Wakefield gazed up at the snowcapped mountains near the large capital building. They had just killed close to one hundred members of the Royal Family on Cootron and many more on the five Battle Cruisers. The Glorious Leader, as was within his personality, would demand revenge for the assassinations. "Or, they will attack us. We need to be prepared."

CHAPTER TEN

Admiral Burton Weems paced the Executive Meeting Room on board the U.N.S.C. *Cortez*. He had many tough decisions to make due to the current events. Many of the top officers from the *Cortez* had been killed and the majority of the crews that he had ordered to serve as temporary crew members on the *Tonkin Gulf* and the *Cleopatra* had ended up being killed in the recent ambush orchestrated by Doctor Sowa and his partners.

Weems examined the faces of Lincoln, Marywood, Tony Allen, Jin-Woo, Malveaux, Murdock, engineer Danica Garcia and Lieutenant Hans Streicher.

"How much longer until we arrive at planet Cootron?" Weems asked, his voice sounded fatigued.

"Less than twenty hours sir," Streicher announced.

Weems nodded and sat down, "Lieutenant Commander Marywood, I am going to field promote you to the rank of Captain and assign you to be the commander of the Battle Cruiser Cleopatra. Shigeta is already on board there so he can act as your first officer. I also field promote Tony Allen to serve as Captain of the Tonkin Gulf. I am ordering that Doctor Jin-Woo be the First Officer of the Cortez. Since Captain Sowa and Lieutenant Brown are out of commission due to those micro-chip implants in their heads, I need a security chief on the Cortez. Lieutenant Murdock, I am field promoting you to MI rank of Captain and you will be filling that slot. Since most of our casualties seemed to be in either the Marines or engineering, our options are slim. Murdock, you will need to have Sergeant Light from the Marines serve as your second in command until further notice."

"Yes, Admiral." Murdock said without emotion. She knew she was the last of the Sikorsky clan on the *Cortez*. The idiot Laurent Sowa had screwed up his hostile takeover attempt on the *Cleopatra* and *Tonkin Gulf*. All Sowa managed to accomplish was get himself, Goodman, Urbanczyk and Anastasia killed in the failed coup attempts. Murdock wished they had waited until they arrived on Cootron to begin the attacks. But it was too late for second guessing the events of the past. Murdock had to deal with the hand she was dealt.

The meeting broke up and each of the officers and

doctors began to move on to their new destinations. Murdock walked back to the MI offices and saw that Sergeant Major Light was there, typing on his computer pad. He stood when she walked into the room.

"At ease, Sergeant Major." Murdock told him. "Report."

Light sat back in his seat. "Captain Sowa, Lieutenant Brown and the other survivors requiring medical attention have already arrived on the Cortez and are in the Medical area. Professor Brennan is also here, he was complaining of extreme pain in his side and abdomen. The Doctors are checking on him. They are bringing in the ship psychiatrist to examine Captain Sowa for any mental damage from the brain implant."

Murdock nodded and sat in the seat that Captain Sowa used to occupy when she was the Captain of Security on the *Cortez*. Now that duty fell to Murdock. She saw that Light had returned to working on whatever project he had been working on when she entered the room. Light was a solid employee and a good soldier. He would follow orders. Murdock hoped that the rest of the crew would not put together the Sikorsky connection with Sowa, Urbanczyk and Goodman. Murdock had already heard murmurs from other crew members that Anastasia Sikorsky was a Royal

Family member. Murdock did not concern herself with the average crew member catching onto the connection. She worried about Gorski, Harrison, Andolini and Shigeta. If they put two and two together, then they would come for her. Murdock stood and walked over to her personal desk and sat in her chair. She used her fingerprints to open her desk drawers. Inside were several Stun Darts and Flame Darts. She grabbed a hand full of each and put them into her side pockets on her black jacket. If they came for her, Murdock was determined to take as many as she could with her.

Murdock looked over at Light, curling her hair in her right index finger as she watched him. He was typing on his holographic keypad and looking at his screen before him. Light had always been a steady top sergeant for Captain Sowa. When Light was promoted he continued to demonstrate that he understood the mission of the military. He would follow her orders, just as he had Brown in the past. Murdock desperately needed loyal followers. Macinlock was dead, all of her relatives were gone and there were only a few Marines with the implants in their heads that she would be able to activate at the proper time. But she needed more followers if she were to take offensive action. Light was physically fit and had a rugged look about him. His face looked as if he had a bad case of acne when he was younger.

"Enjoy your work," Murdock muttered to herself. She unzipped the front of her Class C uniform just enough to reveal some cleavage.

"Sergeant, can you come over here and help me with something?" Murdock said in a flirtatious manner. She was leaning over her desk so that Light would get an eyeful of her chest. She noticed his eyes were locked on her breasts when he turned to face her.

"Yes ma'am," Light said eagerly. "What do you need?"

On the Battle Cruiser *Tonkin Gulf*, Dominic had been left in command of the ship. He sat in the Captain's chair on the Command Station and looked at the skeleton crew that had been provided to him. Two pilots, a weapons technician and one computer operative. He had LaShondra Lewis on the second floor weapons room and a few technicians in the engineering section on Level Four.

But the large space craft felt like a Ghost Town. He excused himself to take another walk around the ship. His nerves, or perhaps his adrenaline level, kept him from being able to sit still.

Dominic had walked the hallways several times and

the sound of his boots clanging on the metallic floors was eerie to him. Almost as if he expected that something would jump out at him at any second. He had received the digitized message from Dia Cho and Felicia Essex telling him in cryptic terms of their decision to commit treason. Both of the women pleaded with him to go to their four children should something happen to them. Dominic had only seen several text photographs of the four children that he had loaned his sperm to help create. He had pictures of their birth, their birthday celebrations and other milestones, but he had never been introduced to them as their father. He wondered how uncomfortable or awkward it would be for him and the children if he was forced by events to do as Cho and Essex requested.

To complicate matters further, Dominic had never told Harumi that he had been a sperm donor before they had met. He had no doubt that Harumi would be a wonderful mother. She had a good heart and was caring toward all of her friends. They had discussed having children in the future. It was something Harumi had expressed she wanted. But now Dominic wondered if he should have told her of the four children out there that may soon lose their mothers and need their father. The father they had no idea existed.

He had read the news reports of the killings and the arrests on New Edinburgh. He had been able to find Harumi by holo-com and she had assured him that she was safe. He could tell by the tone in her voice that there was more for her to tell him but she had some pressing reason to keep him in the dark. Dominic further contacted his parents and they were also short in their responses as to what was going on in Clovis City. He wished he was back on his home planet, holding Harumi in his arms with all of his family around for one of their wonderful cook outs. He found himself missing each and every one of his siblings, even the pestering Lucius.

Dominic against the wall for the hallway in the weapons section. He listened and thought he could hear the hum of the well-timed engines of the Battle cruiser. He looked to the ceiling and fought back tears by blinking rapidly as he thought of his brother Marco.

"I don't know what Gods are out there. Please, if you are there, bring my brother home safely and watch over Dia and Felicia. They are two of the best friends I have ever had. Helping them both have their children was possibly one of the best things I ever did. I will never regret that I made their dreams of parenthood possible. Protect their children from harm. Watch them and bring them home." He had whispered every word as if he was worried someone in the ship would hear.

But there was no one around.

Dominic smiled and walked toward the stairwell to go back to the Command Station. He had a job to do. He hoped that by keeping himself occupied with work it would take his thoughts off of the danger his brother was plunging into.

CHAPTER ELEVEN

The news of the universal political situation was causing Admiral Burton Weems stress. He took a few pain reliever pills so that he could relax in his quarters. When the news reached him that the *Cortez* had entered the orbit of the planet Cootron, he stood and made certain that his uniform was in good condition before leaving to meet Lincoln on the Command Station. As he walked down the hallways and to the main elevator lift, officer and enlisted men and women would stop and salute him. Weems walked into the command area and saw the Lincoln was waiting for him. Weems saw that pilots Frank Glenn and Hans Streicher were sitting at the astral navigation and pilot seats respectively. There were several computer technicians on the upper two levels that were diligently working.

Weems had been briefed on the loss of Doctor Macinlock and the other dead. He fully understood that if Mara Sowa, Brown and the several Marines did not recover from their surgeries to remove the implants in their brains then his options for field promotions grew thinner. Weems shook Lincoln's hand.

"So, we are finally here." Weems said softly.

"Yes Admiral. Time to put this mystery to an end." Lincoln nodded and pointed at the main view screen that showed the brown and blue colored planet Cootron. "We have made contact with Admiral Cardenas. He is on the planet surface and he has invited all of us to join with him to discuss the current events."

Weems pondered that for a moment. "Jamal, I am not comfortable with us sending down all of our top leaders to meet Cardenas. We do not know what he is up to. Ever since we located his lost ships we have lost valuable crew members and the mystery just gets deeper and deeper. And now with Admiral Khan instituting a blockade around Sikorsky's Planet and calls for replacing the Glorious Leader are popping up all over the Eight Solar systems, we need to proceed with caution."

Doctor Henri Malveaux was listening in and nodded. "Admiral, if I may. I agree with you that things are not as they seem. Doctor Wakefield was an old and dear friend of mine. I know that he is on Cootron with Admiral Cardenas. Perhaps I could go down, as an emissary from our ship, and speak to them face to face."

"That couldn't hurt," Lincoln shrugged as he was a bit surprised that the arrogant Malveaux would volunteer for anything.

Weems directed his gaze at Malveaux for a moment as he thought over the offer. "I agree, Henri. You and I both will go together. You can use your friendship with Wakefield and I will use my past association with Cardenas.   Jamal, instruct Jason Allen to prepare a Raumschiff to take us to the planet surface. Also alert Gorski, Harrison and Murdock that we will need them to come along to lead the security detail. Just in case we need to fight our way back out. Leave Shigeta, Lorbek and Andolini in charge of security on the other ships. If this is a trap I don't want us split up too much."

"Sir, perhaps I should go instead of you." Tony Allen suggested from the executive officer chair. "I could get a feel for what is happening and when the time is right you could join us. Please, Admiral. We don't need for you to walk into a trap."

Weems put his hand on Allen's shoulder. "Thank you, Tony. But, no, it should be me. I know Cardenas very well. I doubt he would do anything against me. Tell Jason Allen to be ready to depart in thirty minutes. It is time to put an end to this mystery."

"Yes, Admiral." Lincoln nodded.

Gorski had always wanted to visit the lovely water-filled Cootron. He had seen thousands of pictures of the planetary mountain ranges that were covered with snow that melted into cascading waterfalls. Even though he had seen more than his share of action since joining the crew, he hoped that he would be requested to lead a landing party on the planet surface. Gorski was in a bed on the battle Cruiser *Cleopatra* making love to Jan Eis Harcourt when the order came for him to rendezvous with Jason Allen and prepare to escort Admiral Weems to the planet surface. Gorski was on top of Jan Eis kissing her lips and running his hands over her cotton white body.

"Don't go yet," Jan Eis pleaded as she wrapped her smooth and shapely legs around Gorski's rear. "I love how it feels when you are inside of me."

Gorski was breathing heavily due to their love making. He wanted to stay with her as well and continued his rhythmic thrusts inside of her. He continued until he felt like he exploded inside of her. They stayed in their position and kissed each other for a few moments until he slowly slid off of her and sat up on the bed.

"I hate to leave, Jan. I wanted to spend the rest of

the day with you."

She sat up next to him and ran her fingers through his hair, "I wanted that, too. But duty calls. Yuri, when you come back I will show you something amazing. Something you have never experienced in your life."

He smiled at that and playfully kissed her. "You have shown me so much."

"I saw your dreams last night," Jan Eis said to him.

"My dreams?" Gorski wondered where she was going with that statement. He also was concerned that she was too comfortable reading his thoughts.

"Yes. Last night you dreamed of me meeting your mother. It was a beautiful dream."

"My mother is dead, Jan."

"I know, you told me. But this dream was powerful, Yuri. I wasn't trying to use my powers on you at all. She spoke to me. It was like we were all three linked together."

"You mean you and I were having the same dream at the same time?"

"All three of us," Jan Eis corrected him. "It was as if all three of us were linked in some way, together. I have never experienced something like it before."

"I don't understand what you are telling me, Jan."

"I have seen spirits before. Ghosts. They have

spoken to me in my dreams. Sometimes I see them while I am awake. Pilots I have met from the outer regions of space call them Astral Angels. Sometimes they reveal themselves and ask that we do things for them. You never heard of them?"

"No. Never."

"Your mother comes to you in your dreams, Yuri. I saw her. I felt her presence all around us. She expressed to me that she is worried about you. She was real. It was a feeling of love, of great peace. She told me to be good to you."

"So then it was your dream and not mine?"

Jan Eis sighed. "Yuri you are not hearing me. Your mother was here. Not physically here. But she was here, in this room with us both. And I could tell that for you it had not been the first time she has visited."

Gorski felt uneasy speaking of the subject. "She died many years ago when I was just a boy. I loved her very much. Sometimes I wake up and I can remember my dreams. I can remember her being in my dreams. My brother has told me he has seen her, too. Maybe she is our guardian angel."

"Yuri she wants you to be careful."

"I will be."

She frowned and took his hand in hers. "Yuri. Do not trust Murdock. I know you have been involved with her. She is a witch and a killer. She has turned people against one another. She has set in motion some bad events that really will affect you in a way that I cannot predict the outcome."

"I never trusted Laura. I enjoyed having sex with her, yes, but I never trusted her. I always felt she was up to something."

"Good." Jan Eis smiled as she had been slightly threatened by Murdock. She was already in love with Gorski and she was glad that Murdock would not be any competition for her. "Yuri, she tried to seduce your friend Dominic."

Gorski began laughing. "Laura did that? I bet he tossed her out on her ass. Harumi would beat Dom down if he messed around with another woman."

"Well, my love. Dom was not the only one she tried to seduce."

Gorski looked into her eyes, "What are you talking about?"

"Your friend, Drew. She seduced him."

Gorski sat in silence for a few minutes until the computerized voice alerted him that he needed to report to the Docking Bay. "Are you certain? Did Drew, did he have sex with her?"

Jan Eis nodded, "I am sorry."

Gorski stood up and found his black Class C uniform. He began dressing without comment. He had confided in Harrison many times that he had desired a relationship with Murdock. Gorski could not understand why Harrison would betray him and Lewis at the same time. He shook his head to himself as he began stepping into his black boots.

"Yuri, please don't hold it against Drew. She drugged him with a topical solution to let down his guard. I can tell you that Drew has been emotionally distraught over it and has wanted to confess it to you many times."

Gorski found his web belt and wrapped it around himself. He began strapping his weapons onto it. "That explains why he has been distant with me. I feel really bad for both Drew and LaShondra. She was in love with him. She must be going through a lot of pain."

"She is," Jan Eis confirmed. It had not been necessary for her to read Lewis' mind to come to that conclusion. It was evident that Lewis was hurt and livid with Harrison any time he would walk in the same room.

Gorski walked to her and kissed her, "I will be back

when I can be."

He walked quickly out of the quarters and ran toward the main staircase. He was running a little late and needed to make up the time. Jason Allen was a prompt fellow and Gorski did not want to keep the man waiting.

Betraying Lewis was never his intention. Drew Harrison had been sitting alone in the Take Ten on board the *Cleopatra*. His guilt over what he did to Lewis and Gorski had pushed him to drinking again. He had a bottle of whiskey on his table and was taking occasional sips from it. Fortunately, the robotic wait staff did not judge him when he refused a glass with the bottle. He had tried to call Julia Steiner on her holo-com but she did not answer. He needed someone to confide in and she had always been a good listener.

His wrist had been repaired with metal parts and he was pretty much healed. There was a scar around his wrist area from the operation. The doctors promised Harrison that the skin would heal and the scar would fade away after time. He looked at his hand and realized how close he came to death in his battle with Anastasia Sikorsky. He lamented that he failed to save Macinlock and the nurses and Marines. She killed so effortlessly and efficiently. The Royal family certainly knew how to make themselves nearly invincible.

"I am such a failure," Harrison said to himself as he took another drink. "All those people dead because I couldn't stop her. What am I doing out here?"

He took another drink.

He heard his holo-com chime and pulled it from his web belt. He listened to the orders from Tony Allen to report to the Docking Bay and join a mission to Cootron. Harrison stood up and corked the bottle. He felt a slight buzz but he was not too drunk to walk. He went back to the room that he was using on the ship, retrieved his laser rifle and pistol and then made his way downstairs to meet Allen.

When Harrison arrived in the Docking Area he saw that Jason Allen, Murdock, Gorski, Light and several Marines were waiting there. They were all carrying laser rifles and smiled when he arrived.

"Move it, Lieutenant." Murdock told him. "We have a mission to complete."

Harrison nodded and walked past her and onto the back ramp to the Raumschiff. He stopped in his tracks when he saw Lewis there talking with Admiral Weems. She cut her eyes at Harrison and looked away from him quickly. She was still broken hearted from his betrayal. Weems seemed to have put a large amount of trust in Harrison's former lover. He heard the Admiral request that she stay by his side at all times.

Harrison said nothing and took a seat and began strapping on his safety harness.

The rest of the mission members walked on board. Gorski sat down next to Harrison and slapped him on the leg.

"You feeling okay, big guy?"

Harrison shook his head, "Not really. I sometimes wish I was somewhere else."

Gorski smiled at him, "Take a breath mint. You still have whiskey on your breath. You started again didn't you?"

Harrison turned his head away from Gorski. He had difficulties with alcohol in the past and Gorski knew about it. He had even tried to convince him to take Antabuse 5X, a drug that made a person vomit if they drank any alcohol. "I don't want to hear it."

"Damn it, Drew." Gorski whispered to him. "We are supposed to be guarding an Admiral. Get your shit together."

Murdock walked over to the two men and smiled.

"How are my two favorite pets doing? Everyone getting along well? Hmmm?"

Harrison said nothing. Gorski tried to keep what he knew about Murdock to himself. "How is everyone doing on the Cortez?"

"Oh we are doing fine," Murdock said with a smile on her face. "I sure miss your hard cock inside of me, Yuri. Perhaps when the mission is completed, you and I could hook up?"

Gorski smiled at her. If he said no, then she would conclude that he knew she was up to no good. "I would love that, Laura."

"Good answer," Murdock told him. "Now, if you will excuse me I am needed upstairs."

Harrison and Gorski watched her leave in silence. They felt the Raumschiff beginning to move as Jason Allen and his co-pilot, Paula Vela, began to guide the space craft out of the Docking Bay. The rear doors to the ship sealed shut before they entered space and began flying toward Cootron.

Gorski could feel the tension toward him from Harrison. He finally looked over at his friend. "Drew, what is wrong?"

Harrison sighed and turned his head toward Gorski.

"I'm a fuck up, Yuri. I couldn't stop Anastasia and all those people died because I failed them. I almost died. She killed all those people, even the sleeping Marines. I couldn't stop her. I couldn't stop her."

He buried his face in his hands and sighed again.

"Nobody could stop her, Drew. She killed all of the weapons crew, too. Wiped them out." Gorski put his hand on Harrison's shoulder. "You did save some people by your actions, Drew. Two nurses are alive today because of your actions. Stop beating yourself up over it."

"You stopped her," Harrison shot back. "You knew what to do and I didn't."

"Is that why you started drinking again?"

Harrison was silent for about three minutes. He wanted desperately to tell his friend what had happened. He finally decided to do as his mother always taught him. Tell the truth. "Yuri, I slept with Laura Murdock. I don't know why I did it. She came to my room and it just happened. I know you wanted her, and I know that I violated our trust to not mess with each other's woman. That is why I am drinking, Yuri. I am drinking again because I betrayed my best friend and in doing so I broke LaShondra's heart. I hurt her really bad. I am such a fuck up Yuri. I shouldn't be here. I should be off in a different career. One where I won't get people hurt or killed. I messed up everything for myself and the two people I love the most. LaShondra will never forgive me and I know you won't either."

Gorski shook his head, "That's where you are wrong, Drew. I do forgive you. Laura is not the kind of woman you marry. She's a user. She used you and she used me. She plays games with men. She is dangerous in that she has a fantastic body and a face that would launch a thousand ships. But you know what, I doubt I would have been able to tell her no if the situation was reversed. She is one of those women that most men cannot deny. You are my best friend, Drew and I do forgive you. You hear me?"

Harrison had tears rolling down his cheeks. "I have felt so guilty about it. For days, I didn't know how to tell you what I had done. You are too good a friend to me, Yuri."

The two men embraced as Harrison felt the weight of some of his guilt go away. But his feelings regarding what he did to Lewis were crushing him with emotional turmoil. He was relieved that he did not lose his best friend.

In the pilot section, Jason Allen flew the Raumschiff into the atmosphere of planet Cootron. Vela was checking coordinates on the computer panel before them and monitoring the scanners to make sure there were no offensive weapons coming their way. Vela had gotten her orders to attend the mission while she was in the shower. She had thrown on her dark blue flight suit without taking the time to dry off. Her hair was still wet and her uniform was clinging to her body. Vela thought she caught Allen checking her out a few times during the flight. She had always been attracted to Allen but nothing had ever come of it due to the meddling Laura Murdock.

Vela kept her mind on her job as they began to receive transmissions from the planet surface. It was from Admiral Cardenas.

"Welcome to Cootron!" Cardenas told them. "I will send you the coordinates of the landing pad where we will rendezvous. Please tell Admiral Weems that we have much to discuss. I look forward to our meeting."

"You think we are walking into a trap?" Vela asked.

Allen shook his head, "After everything we have seen and been through, I would not be surprised by anything. I for one want to hear what has to be said. We have lost so many crew members, Paula. French lost his wife. He is so lost with pain. I cannot imagine loving someone that much and losing her like that."

"Have you ever loved a woman like French loved her?"

Allen looked at Vela for a few seconds. He had always found her to be pleasant and insightful over the time he served on the *Cortez* with her. He also found her attractive, especially with the way her uniform was clinging to her while she was wet. He had never seen Vela with a serious relationship, which was understandable given the huge woman to man ratio in the population. Allen pursed his lips together and thought that he would see if she had any interest in him. After the laser fights he had just participated in there was one thing he was certain of and that was the old saying that life is too short. "No. But I think that I could. But I never could tell if she was interested in me that way."

Vela looked away from Allen and at her computer panel. She had hoped that one day Allen would give her a chance. She was certain she was not his type. Murdock was blonde, white skinned with an amazing body. Vela was Hispanic with dark hair and olive skin tone. She was shorter than Murdock and not as well endowed. Plus, Allen was from one of the wealthiest families in the Eight Solar Systems. Vela was an average girl from an average family. She was certain that his family would never approve of her due to her lack of financial status. She was curious though to find out who it was that Jason Allen had his eyes on. "Is it someone we know?"

"Yes. You." Allen said softly.

Vela felt her heart jump in her chest. "You mean you want, you want to be involved with me?"

Allen nodded, "I think you are a great gal, Paula Vela. Yeah. I would like for us to see if there could be anything between us. That is if you would be willing to take a chance on a spoiled rich boy like me?"

Vela tried to suppress her smile. "I would like that very much, Jason. I think that you are, great, too. So what do we do now?"

"We do what any other potential couple would do." Allen told her. "We make a date for dinner and get to know each other better."

Vela smiled, "So you want to wine and dine me?"

"Absolutely."

Weems relaxed on the second level of the Raumschiff with Malveaux, Murdock and Lewis. The rest of the Marines were scattered about the ship. Weems thought he noticed Murdock glaring at Lewis and that

Lewis was ignoring the other woman. He sensed a tension there. Weems quickly picked up his communication device and began dictating orders for his personal reports for the Space Command. He did not know what to expect when they landed. But he was glad he had Lewis, Light and Murdock there to protect him.

Jason Allen had spent the flight down talking with Vela about the large mountains on Cootron and the spectacular waterfalls that they would see due to the snow caps melting. She watched with her eyes wide open as Allen flew the ship toward a high rise building.

"We're landing there?" Vela asked.

Allen nodded, "That was the coordinates we got from Admiral Cardenas. It is one of the government buildings."

"It is massive," Vela observed. "What is it about one hundred floors high?"

"At least," Allen said. "It was built into the side of the mountain range next to it. You will see how it is connected when we fly around the east side of it. The mountain is named Allen's Peak, after my great grandfather. It is higher than the tallest mountain on old Earth. My family has a few large factories on this planet so I spent some time here as a kid. The water is so pure that you can drink it without using any filtration devices. I hope we get to stay for a while so I can show you some of the nicer locations. I see the landing strip on the roof. It is big enough to land five Raumschiff's on it. Let the crew know we are landing."

Vela smiled and began to speak into the ship communication system to have everyone strap in their safety harnesses and prepare for landing. She could see a group of about thirty people waiting for them on the landing pad and waiving in their direction. Vela had a laser pistol attached to her web belt. She thought that she might not need the weapon after all.

Admiral Cardenas had selected about thirty individuals to accompany him and greet his old friend, Admiral Weems. Among the welcoming party were Knox, Wakefield, Skye Sikorsky, Rima al-Bashir, Military Intelligence Lieutenant Maxwell Rochford, Space Command Lieutenant Analisa Williamson, several of the Replicants of Love-Easter, Garrison and Penella. They waived their hands at the Raumschiff as Jason Allen softly set the ship down for a safe landing.

Rochford was a taller man with dark hair and slim build. He had been in the service for seven years and acted as Admiral Cardenas' personal body guard ever since the war with the Royal family began. Rochford had been born and raised on Sikorsky's Planet and had a wife and three children.

Williamson was the personal pilot to Admiral Cardenas and had his every confidence. She was also one of his secret lovers. She was about seven inches over five feet tall and had dark hair and eyes. She had a small scar on her left cheek from a knife fight years ago. She would always tell others that her opponent in that fight got worse. She had no husband or children but numerous brothers and sisters back on planet New Berlin. Williamson was a decent translator as she could speak seven languages fluently.

Admiral Weems nodded to Lewis, Murdock and Light when the ship came to a full stop. "Time to go."

"Admiral, allow us to go out first with our Marines and survey the situation," Light told him.

Murdock nodded, "I agree with the Sergeant Major. You and Doctor Malveaux should wait for us to go first."

Weems motioned for the exit and allowed Light to lead the Marines out to the loading dock exit. They found Gorski and Harrison there waiting. Both men had laser rifles ready.

Murdock ordered for the ship computer to lower the back loading bay door. The group waited patiently as the door slowly opened and the ramp slid to the landing pad. By now Vela and Allen had joined the group. Both of the pilots were modestly armed in comparison to the others, bearing only laser pistols. As soon as the walking ramp hit the ground, Light led seven Marines out first, followed by Murdock and then Gorski and Harrison.

Harrison saw the mountains to the rear and wanted to comment on their beauty. He kept his comments to himself as he was on duty. He looked over the welcoming party and recognized the Love-Easter Replicants immediately as they did him.

"Drew!" One of the Love-Easter clones said as he ran to him. "It is so good to see you again! How have you been?"

Another of the Love-Easters recognized Gorski and moved toward him. "Yuri! My friend you look amazing! I am so glad that you are here!"

Gorski and Harrison were stunned by the sight of multiple copies of one of their dearest friends. Before they could start asking too many questions, one of the Love-Easter clones explained the truth behind their existence. They were stunned by the explanation of how so many Love-Easters were present.

"Just how many of you are there?" Harrison finally

asked.

"About a thousand," one of the Love-Easters told them.

"And the one that married Yesenia?" Gorski wanted to know.

"He is one of us. He was chosen to be the one to live as the real Drayton. The rest of us are our own person but we are committed to eliminating the Sikorsky's as we hope that you will agree with our mission and join us."

Skye Sikorsky narrowed her eyes when she saw Murdock. She knew that she had seen her face before but could not place it.

Knox approached Gorski and held out his hand. "Hello young man. You probably don't remember me. Your father served under me many years ago when you were only six years old. How is your father doing?"

Gorski shook the extended hand from Knox. "I do remember you sir. You gave my father his first promotion and his first two medals. My father is well, thank you. You look well yourself. How are your children?"

"Some are here, others in different locations. But everyone is healthy. So you went in to MI service? Good career choice. We all knew you would make a fine officer when we saw you on that Blood Moon."

Gorski noticed the Ella Ragnarsson duplicates in the distance. He instinctively aimed his laser rifle in their direction. "Sir, do you know who that is?"

"Don't worry, they are with us," Knox told him. "They are clones. Just like the Love-Easter's you met. The Ella clones have a different set of memories in them. You see the body of Ragnarsson, but she is another person entirely."

"I don't think I follow, sir." Gorski whispered.

"Neither do I," Knox laughed. "But I just play along. Try to do the same. The Ella clones are no threat, I promise."

Gorski nodded but resolved himself to keep at least one eye on them.

Murdock walked around the large landing area and looked over the edge and surveyed the mountains to the south. She noted that the drop off from the landing pad was about one hundred thirty floors. Anyone that fell from that height would be dead for certain. There were no signs of any assassins or waiting soldiers to ambush them. She nodded for Admiral Weems to approach. She watched as Weems and Cardenas hugged each other. Out of the corner of her eye, Murdock noticed Skye Sikorsky looking her over. Murdock realized that the woman had a familiarity about her that she could not place. She acted as if she had not noticed the other woman and began thinking of her face while she strained to listen to the words of Admiral Cardenas.

Allen and Vela stood back on the loading ramp of the Raumschiff, watching everyone closely.

"Burton, I am glad you have come."

"I am happy to be here my old friend," Weems told him.

Malveaux and Wakefield shook hands when they saw one another. They were exchanging pleasantries back and forth as the Admiral's negotiated.

"Burton, we have problems with the Royal Family." Cardenas began.

"What sort of problems?"

"The Royals have been kidnaping and enslaving people for almost two hundred years for one horrible and ugly purpose."

"Which was what?"

"To cut them open and steal their body parts for themselves," Cardenas responded. "They have had thousands of slaves and they have them to this very day.

Not just the alien slaves that were on the Blood Moon, but humans as well. The Rosenburg's that were on the Blood Moon. The ones that caused the death of my son? They were Royal's. I have proof of that fact. I also have proof that Vladimir Sikorsky helped them kill my son."

Weems had known Cardenas for almost his entire professional life. Cardenas was not a liar nor did he exaggerate. For Weems, the proof was not important. The fact that Cardenas believed the accusations was the most critical piece of information for him.

"We have much more information, the same information Admiral Khan and Captain Allen were given. I decided to take my forces and liberate Cootron from the Sikorsky's. His Royal Family members on board my Battle Cruisers fought us and we had to abandon the Cleopatra and Tonkin Gulf back where you found them."

"That explains some things," Weems said. "What about the headless bodies?"

"That is the only way to kill a Royal effectively," Rima al-Bashir answered. "Each Royal has a microchip that has been placed in their brain. When they die, the microchip has a complete and accurate copy of all their thoughts, memories, education, and experiences. Everything that is them is in that chip. The sensation of death caused the microchip to send, or upload all of those brain patterns to one of hundreds of orbital satellites. Then those patterns are downloaded into a clone that is waiting in some undisclosed location. That clone receives the memories and everything and is activated. The Royal then rises to live again."

"So why the decapitations?" Weems shook his head trying to understand.

"Because the decapitation of a Royal stops that process. The microchip, for some reason will not activate unless the cause of death is something else. Severing the head does not send the proper nerve response to start the uploading process," Cardenas explained. "We had no choice but to do it that way. Otherwise the Royal would wake up in some other location, inside a cloned body and be able to report to the other Royals what had happened."

Weems was stunned by the information he was receiving. He looked over at the several Replicants of Love-Easter, Garrison and Ella. "Are they what you call Replicants?"

"Yes," Cardenas answered. "They are perfect copies of the original host. Only the woman there only has the physical body of the Ragnarsson assassin. Her brain patterns are from someone else."

"I don't believe it," Weems said as he studied the faces of the clones.

Malveaux approached the two Admirals with Wakefield at his side.

"Believe it," Malveaux said. "They have explained everything to me and it is possible. Hell, it is. We see the proof before us. I think we should join them, Admiral."

Weems looked around and saw that Light had positioned his Marines strategically around them. Murdock was across the landing pad from Light and she was watching everything in silence. Gorski and Harrison were alert but were being distracted by one of the Love-Easter Replicants. He thought over what Cardenas, al-Bashir and Malveaux had told him. He compared their story with everything they found since locating the *Cleopatra* and the *Tonkin Gulf*. He had more questions.

"Join them? What exactly would we be joining?" Weems wanted to know.

"The revolution," Cardenas said simply. "You would be aligning yourself with us and going out to join Admiral Khan to overthrow the Glorious Leader."

"So we would be committing treason?" Weems concluded.

"One man's traitor is another's hero," Malveaux

said softly. "Sir, I know I rarely speak up. But the Glorious Leader has lived for over two hundred forty years. Think about it. That is not natural. There is truth to what they are saying."

Weems looked over his shoulder and saw that Lewis was behind him covering his back. "Corporal, what do you think?"

"Me, sir?" Lewis was surprised that an Admiral would ask her what her opinion was.

"Yes, you. You were there when Urbanczyk and Sowa went crazy. You saw all of the crew members that had died. You saw when Andolini had to fight those men with those new weapons. Your opinion matters very much to me. Forget that I am an Admiral and that you are a Corporal. Speak to me soldier to soldier. Human being to human being. What do you think?"

Lewis looked the Admiral in the eye. "Sir, freedom is a beautiful thing. I also was there on New Edinburgh when the Rosenburg family was able to walk all over anyone they wanted to. That is until Yuri and Drew over there took a stand against them. I say it is time for a new direction. I think the people deserve to choose their leaders and not have them forced on them. I say we go join Admiral Khan and light their butts on fire."

"You would be willing to fight and die to overthrow the Glorious Leader?" Weems pressed her.

"Yes sir, I would." Lewis said boldly. "Sir, I saw innocent weapons technicians cut down by those people. They are sadistic and they think of us as lab rats. I want no man or woman being my leader that has that low of an opinion of me. Sir."

"Then that is good enough for me," Weems looked at Cardenas in the eye. "I cannot speak for all of my people. Each man and woman must make their own choice. If we are striving for change, then it starts here and now. I will ask all my people to vote on whether or not they wish to be a part of your rebellion. I will never ask anyone under my command to do something that I am not also willing to do. If my crew says no, will you let us go in peace?"

"You know that I will, Burton." Cardenas told him. "Anyone that does not wish to participate does not have to."

Murdock heard every word and was now seething with rage. The discussion of her family was all she could take. With her laser rifle in her hands she had her lips curled back in anger she decided that the time to act was now.

"Traitors," Murdock hissed. She motioned to Light

that it was time. She had previously arranged with Light and her security forces that if there were any talks of rebellion that they were to kill the traitors. Light nodded that he understood and he motioned for his Marines to open fire.

Lewis heard the scream of agony from Admiral Weems when the laser blast fired by Murdock ripped into his chest. Some of Weems' blood and body matter splattered in Lewis' face. She watched in horror as Weems was thrown violently to the ground and his body slid for several feet until it slammed into the protective barricade around the landing pad.

Admiral Cardenas also was hit by a blast from Light. The Admiral flipped head over heels from the force to the shot and landed on his stomach with a thud. Rima al-Bashir also went down, her left arm severed from her body.

Lewis cursed as she jumped to the ground and began firing her laser rifle back at Light and the other Marines. Gorski and Harrison also hit the ground and began looking for targets to fire back at. Gorski noticed from the corner of his eye that Knox was hit and fell to the ground. One of the Love-Easter clones never had time to seek cover as his head was vaporized by a laser blast.

Vela and Allen narrowly missed being hit by shots

fired at them by the Marines. Both of the pilots dived onto the metal floor of the Raumschiff as laser beams sliced through the air over their heads. Vela drew her laser pistol as she rolled behind the walls of the ship. She saw that Allen had done the same on the other side.

Murdock was moving forward toward the exit from the landing area. Her plan was to get into the building and make a break for it. Skye Sikorsky was determined to prevent her escape and jumped on Murdock's back. The professor was no challenge for a trained MI officer. Murdock grabbed Skye by her hair and arm and then flipped her hard to the ground. Skye was stunned by the impact and could not block the incoming kick from Murdock. Skye was unconscious after Murdock's boot slammed into her face.

Murdock then moved forward firing her laser rifle with deadly precision. She dispatched two of the Garrison Replicants with direct shots to their chests. Both flipped spastically to the ground as they died soon after they were hit. Murdock saw that Williamson had her laser pistol drawn and was running toward the downed Admirals. Murdock fired one blast at her and watched with glee as Williamson's head was splattered in every direction, her headless body staggered around in circles for a few seconds before sliding to the ground.

Rochford pulled out a laser pistol and was charging at Murdock and she fired two shots at him. The man screamed as his stomach and back were blown open. His body spun around and hit the ground. Murdock ran over his body and made it to the exit doors.

Gorski and Harrison were helping Lewis fire back at Light and the other Marines. The Love-Easter and Penella Replicants were doing the same. From the Raumschiff, Vela and Allen were firing in support of Lewis. Vela aimed and fired at Light, hitting him in the shoulder. Light screamed and fell backwards over the protective barricade. He screamed as he fell over one hundred thirty floors to his death. None of the combatants heard the crunch of his bone when his body was scattered on the rocky surface below.

"Yuri!" Jason Allen screamed pointing at the exit toward Murdock. "We got this! Get her!"

Gorski and Harrison looked over their shoulders and saw that Murdock was shooting one of the Penella Replicants point blank range.

"You with me?" Gorski asked.

"Let's kill that bitch," Harrison affirmed.

Gorski stood and began running at full speed to the

doorway with Harrison right behind him. One of the Love-Easter Replicants joined them and was right behind Harrison. The Love-Easter clone did not make it as he was hit in the back by a laser blast causing the front of his chest to explode outward. Pieces of his flesh and rib cage littered the ground.

Murdock realized that the two men she had been sleeping with were charging after her. She pulled out two thermite grenades and tossed them behind her as she ran. She found a stairwell to the left and desperately pushed opened the door. An attractive woman was standing before her holding a briefcase and a cup of coffee in her other hand.   She gave Murdock and inquisitive look just before Murdock fired her laser point blank at her and blew a hole in her chest. The woman flew backwards from the power of the laser and was dead before she hit the ground. Her coffee spilled on the floor and was dripping down the stairs.

Murdock entered the stairwell and began descending as fast as she could run.

Gorski saw the two grenades on the ground and stopped, grabbed Harrison by the arm and flung him to the ground. The grenades ignited and brightened the entire scene. Gorski stood up and saw that Harrison was pushing himself up with a look on his face of rage. Gorski ran past the exit doors and saw several civilians screaming in fear as he rushed past them.

"The woman!" Harrison yelled at one of the civilian workers. "Where did she go?"

"The stairwell," a woman in business attire answered, pointing at the door that Murdock had gone through.

Gorski and Harrison ran to the door and pushed it open. The only way to go was down. Gorski took the point and began descending with Harrison behind him. Both had their laser rifles ready, aiming downward. Gorski was certain he could hear Murdock's footsteps below. She was running fast. Gorski began to run faster. His only goal was to make Murdock pay for the people she had just killed.

Lewis, Vela, Allen, and the remaining Replicants of Love-Easter, Ella and Garrison continued the laser battle with the remaining Marines. Lewis was able to sever one of the Marines legs off, just below her knees. She dropped her rifle and was on the ground screaming in agony. One of the laser shots fired by Allen hit one Marine in the chest, sending the man falling over the wall as Light had done. The tide in the battle turned in favor of Lewis and her shipmates as one by one the Marines fell, dying or injured from laser wounds.

During the entire battle, Malveaux had intentionally fallen on top of Wakefield and covered his friend with his body. Miraculously, neither scientist was hit in the crossfire.

The two doctors were up and checking the injured. Knox was on the ground with his left leg shot off from just above the knee. Wakefield checked the pulse rates of al-Bashir, Cardenas and Weems. He looked to Lewis and the two pilots. "Help me! These four all need immediate medical attention!"

Vela and Allen did not hesitate as they holstered their laser pistols and ran down the ramp to lend a hand. Lewis helped Malveaux lift up Knox while the surviving Replicants helped with Cardenas, Skye and al-Bashir. Vela and Allen carefully lifted Weems and followed Wakefield into the building. Vela could see through Weems chest and smell the scent of his burned flesh. She turned her head away and fought the urge to vomit.

Gorski jumped backwards when Murdock fired up at him. The laser blast missed Gorski's head by five inches and burned a black scorch mark into the wall of the stairwell. Gorski concluded he was too close for comfort for Murdock. He fired back and heard his laser rifle shot hit the wall. Murdock kept running downward.

Harrison was breathing heavily from all the running. "That bitch is fast."

"We both have seen her naked. She has no fat on her and has good muscle tone. She is in great shape. We gotta move faster!" Gorski urged. "We can't let her escape. Come on. Keep up."

Gorski kept running full speed and had to slide down a flight of stairs as Murdock had positioned herself at the corner of the floor landing and was firing a volley of laser blasts at him. Gorski, by sliding as he had, narrowly missed having his head blown off. He gritted his teeth from the pain of his back sliding down the metal stairs.

Harrison noticed that Murdock had all of her attention on Gorski. He aimed his laser rifle carefully and smiled. He had Murdock in his sights. Murdock looked up at Harrison and saw that he was aiming at her. She screamed.

Harrison pulled the trigger.

The laser blast hit Murdock in the chest and blew a basketball size hole out of her back. Her body flipped backwards and rolled down the next flight of stairs. Harrison could see Murdock's blood all over the wall where she had been standing in front of before he shot her.

Harrison ran to his friend and helped him to his feet. Gorski and Harrison ran to Murdock and saw she was not moving. Gorski kicked her over, face up. Her eyes were wide open, staring at nothing. Her once beautiful face that had lured numerous men to bed was covered with blood. She was clearly dead.

"Fucking bitch," Harrison said of Murdock.

Gorski started laughing and Harrison did as well. The two men hugged each other.

"Come on," Gorski said. "Let's get back upstairs and see how badly they hurt us."

"I need a drink," Harrison told him.

"No you don't."

Planet Cootron was firmly under the control of Rear Admiral Cardenas and retired General Knox. The citizens were dancing in the streets and rejoicing at the news of the one sided victory and their deliverance from the rule of the cruel Sikorsky's. Many believed that the battle proved that Sikorsky was weak and that the time had come to oust him as the leader of humanity.

But the crowds did not realize that many of their liberators had been shot down by Murdock and the Marines she had manipulated into doing her dirty work. Wakefield had done his best to save all the victims. Skye Sikorsky lost two teeth but would live. Knox survived but lost a leg. Rima al-Bashir also survived but lost an arm. Cardenas had also survived but was connected to life support as his heart and lungs were damaged and he needed transplant surgery.

Gorski, Malveaux, Harrison, Lewis, Vela and Allen were saddened to learn that Admiral Burton Weems did not survive his wounds. Lewis wept as she had grown fond of the man. He had treated her as an equal, regardless of their difference in rank. Harrison attempted to comfort her but she shunned him, her eyes flashed with anger in his direction due to the memory of his betrayal. The group had been told to wait for Colonel Lincoln to arrive to assess the situation.

Murdock and her Marines had done their damage. In addition to killing Weems they had managed to kill over twenty other people/Replicants and injured four. The medical center of the massive one hundred thirty floor high building had been on floors twenty through thirty. Jason Allen had been kind enough to go to the lower level cafeteria on a coffee run for the others. He returned with a tray holding twelve cups of coffee. He passed them out one by one.

Several of the other officers serving under Cardenas had arrived to pray for their leader. It was a sad and somber moment. Many were crying and some were speechless.

Gorski sat and sipped his coffee and looked out the windows of the twenty-fifth floor. He noticed that Vela and Allen were huddled in a far corner of one of the hallways, talking and sipping coffee. Harrison was pacing up and down a hallway.

Wakefield and Malveaux approached Gorski.

"I am sorry about your Admiral," Wakefield said softly. His white hospital uniform was covered in blood. "The wound was too severe and I couldn't save him."

"I suppose this means the rebellion is over," Malveaux observed. "Without Weems and Cardenas, there is no one left to lead against Sikorsky."

"Colonel Lincoln could," Gorski said.

Malveaux shook his head, "No. He could if it were a ground battle. He would be great for that. But this is something that requires knowledge of space warfare. Lincoln is not the person to lead us."

"Son," Wakefield put his hand on Gorski's shoulder. "I got word from New Edinburgh. The Glorious Leader arrested your father. They murdered his assistant, a man named Evart. They are arresting and killing all kinds of influential people on that planet."

"My father...." Gorski looked out the window, his

hands balled up into fists. "Is he alive?"

Wakefield nodded, "Yes. They cannot kill him yet, at least not until they get rid of all the others on their hit list. And they are doing a good job of it. They have an order to shoot to kill your brother and all of Evart's daughters. They even murdered the entire flight school staff of instructors."

"Admiral Seward?"

"Yes, I regret to inform you that they killed him, too."

"I have to get back there!" Gorski yelled and began to move away from the window. Both Malveaux and Wakefield restrained him by holding his arms.

"Son, they will kill you on sight if you go back there," Wakefield warned him. "We can hide you here, on Cootron. You will be safe here."

"But my father and brother will not be safe!" Gorski yelled. By now Harrison was standing by him. He helped hold Gorski in place.

"He's right," Malveaux added. "You would be walking into a pit of venomous snakes if you go back to New Edinburgh now. Think about it. What are you going to do? Steal a space craft and fly across several solar systems to arrive on planet New Edinburgh? Even if you made it there you would get shot out of the sky seconds after entering the atmosphere. The battle to be fought for the people of New Edinburgh needs to be fought at another location."

"My father, my brother and all of my friends are all back there in danger. I have to do something."

"Yuri, listen to me." Harrison pleaded. "I just spoke with Stella Andolini via holo-com. She told me her family is hiding Piotr and the Evart girls. Piotr is safe. He is safe."

"And my dad?"

Harrison looked down into Gorski's eyes. "He is incarcerated with Captain Tierney and some of the General Assembly Representatives. They won't kill your father for fear that it will spark a riot in Clovis City. But if you go there, they will kill you."

"So we do nothing?" Gorski was beside himself with anger.

"Oh we will do something, young man." It was the voice of Colonel Jamal Lincoln. He was walking down the hallway toward them. Next to him was Lieutenant Jake Brown and Lieutenant Junior Grade Juan Aceto.

Brown had a scar on the back of his head that was two inches long due to the surgery he had gone through to remove the microchip that Laurent Sowa has used to control him. He seemed to be fully recovered from his ordeal as he was walking upright and smiling. He was dressed in his military uniform which meant he had been cleared for duty by the ships surgeons.

"Jake!" Harrison smiled. "You are okay?"

Brown nodded and smiled. "Yes, thank you. I have contacted Dominic and thanked him a million times for not killing me. The doctors took that damn implant out of my head. I am all back to normal now except for the scar they left on the back of my skull."

"And we need to make plans for war," Lincoln said. "I am taking over Cardenas' fleet and we will be joining Admiral Khan to strengthen the blockade around Sikorsky's Planet. I have seen enough to realize that when my daughter Mary returns from her mission to find the Bismark she will find a new world waiting for her. I owe it to her."

"But my family on New Edinburgh needs help." Gorski protested.

"And the best help we can give them is by forcing the Glorious Leader to step down. Are you with me?" Lincoln asked Gorski.

"I have to go to my father," Gorski blurted out.

Lincoln looked at the others and sighed. "Gorski,

walk with me. Just you and I. Come on."

Gorski hesitated as Lincoln put his arm around his shoulder. He led Gorski down the hallway until they were far enough away from the others.

"Yuri, I know that you were sleeping with my daughter for all those years you were together at the Academy," Lincoln began. "Most fathers would not like the idea of their daughter being so active sexually, but I didn't mind. You know why? Because Mary would tell me how you treated her. She told me how kind and good you were. I realized she was in love with you and I was happy for her. When she decided to break up with you I tried to talk her out of it. You know why?"

"No, sir. Why did you?" Gorski wanted to know.

"Because good men are hard to find. I knew my Mary would regret losing you. Yuri, the world watched you and Drew and your other friends do some things when you fought on that Blood Moon. The world saw courage. They saw the willingness to sacrifice for others. They saw bonds of friendship. I saw a group of cadets that were willing to fight to the death and you and your friends were resourceful enough to find a way to live when you should have died. You gave me my Mary back. Eight of ten lived from your team when you all should have died. You know what that told me?"

"No sir."

"It told me that I want you on my side in a dog fight. The Glorious Leader must go, Yuri. I need men like you to help me accomplish that goal. There are eight solar systems of people and other races that want to rid themselves of Sikorsky so badly that they can taste it. I plan on trying to make it a reality. Your father will not be touched by the forces of Sikorsky out of fear of rebellion on the planet. Hell, they may get a rebellion anyway for killing Seward, Evart, Hsu and Goldsmith. But if we can bring Sikorsky to his knees, then your father will be released from jail. You understand me?"

Gorski sighed and realized the Colonel still had his arm around him. "What are you proposing, sir?"

"We give the Battle Cruisers to Admiral Khan to command. You, Shigeta, Harrison, Andolini, Brown, Lewis and me, we are military professionals. We are not pilots. We are going to lead a ground invasion of Sikorsky's Planet and take over the main military and political bases of operation. Are you with me?"

Gorski looked into Lincoln's eyes. "Sir, I always loved your daughter Mary. She was one of the best things that ever happened in my life. She always told me how much she loved and respected you. I know that she learned her values of kindness from you. So, for her, for my father and brother, I am in. I will follow you wherever you direct me to go. Let's go to war."

"That's my boy. Now let's go talk with the others. I have several announcements to make to everyone."

Lincoln led Gorski back to where Wakefield and the others were waiting.

"Well, Yuri? Are we going back to New Edinburgh?" Harrison asked.

"No. We are going with Colonel Lincoln to Sikorsky's Planet," Gorski told his friend. "That is if you are with us?"

Harrison gave Gorski a bear hug. He had hoped that his friend would make the smart choice. "Are you kidding me? Of course I'm in! You and I are best friends and I cannot imagine you fighting in a war like this without me."

Lincoln ordered Aceto to go and get the Raumschiff ready. He turned to face Vela and Allen. "I cannot order any person to commit treason. Lieutenant Vela, I plan on taking an offensive incursion to Sikorsky's Planet. If you wish to take part in it, I could use every good pilot I can get my hands on. How about it?"

Vela smiled at Lincoln, "Sir, you don't even have to

ask. I will be honored to go into battle for you."

Lincoln shook her hand. He turned his attention to Allen. "Jason, before we began our search for the Cleopatra you had submitted your papers for retirement. Clearly you have over stayed your time by a few weeks. I think you should catch a transport here and make your way back to your home on Old Earth. I know we will all wish you the best. You were an excellent pilot and a good officer."

Allen looked over the faces of Gorski, Vela, Harrison, Brown, Lewis, Wakefield, Malveaux and the Replicants of Love-Easter, Garrison and Ella Ragnarsson. "Colonel, when you sent me to the Cleopatra and the Tonkin Gulf I saw several of my shipmates dead. They were my friends. I can't get those memories out of my head and today I saw Admiral Weems, a man I respected, murdered by a Sikorsky. You said you need good pilots, Colonel. I would be honored to fly each one of you into that battle. I think my place is with each of you."

Lincoln grinned and slapped Allen on the shoulder. "Welcome aboard, Lieutenant. Now, Corporal Lewis. You have shown some amazing leadership abilities and a knack for survival. I need more platoon leaders so I am field promoting you from Corporal to Second Lieutenant. You will be leading a platoon for me. Think you can handle that?"

Lewis nodded and swallowed hard. "Yes sir. I will do my best."

"Then let's all load up and get back to the Battle Cruisers. We have a long journey ahead of us."

"Colonel Lincoln!" Wakefield spoke up, "With all due respect, sir. I would like to go along. I spent some time on Sikorsky's Planet. I know some of the terrain and I am very familiar with the major cities. You could use someone like me."

"What about your oath as a doctor to do no harm?"

"I'll leave the fighting to you and your soldiers. I will be there strictly as an advisor and as a surgeon if I am needed."

"All right, Doctor. Get packed and meet us up topside. We leave in fifteen minutes," Lincoln told Wakefield.

"And you will need some of the Replicants that are here," Wakefield added. "They are committed to the cause and have proven to be extremely resourceful and capable in battle. We also have thousands of civilians that are prepared to fight."

"We will need all the allies we can find, Doctor." Lincoln nodded. "Get them ready to join us on the

Raumschiff."

Lincoln walked away from the others without any further comment. He was filled with grief over the death of his friend Burton Weems. For Lincoln, removing Sikorsky had as much to do with avenging Weems and their other dead crew members as it did for a new beginning.

"Good bye old friend," Lincoln said under his breath as he left the hospital ward.

To be continued in Book Three of the Red Javelin Chronicles: *Doctrine of Avoidance*